Human Resource

A Happy Holiday Short

Aria Daze

Daze Dream Publications

Contents

CONTENT WARNINGS

This book contains themes that may be distressing to some readers. Please review the following information before diving in. Your mental health matters!

- Sexual activity

- Deceit (surprise planning.)

- Cursing

- Alcohol use

- Slang (Yes, them folks be using ebonics. Please do not email me about it.)

- Public Sex

- Soft Domination

If this is your jam, please continue onward, dear reader! If not, please consider checking out other books in my catalog.

Dedicated to all the Ho, Ho, Ho's. Have a Holly Jolly Christmas.

To the short kings: You are handsome and loved.

THE PLAYLIST

Scan The QR code to open Spotify!

1. Santa Baby- Eartha Kitt

2. All I Want For Christmas Is You- Mariah Carey

3. Sleigh Ride- TLC

4. Have Yourself A Merry Little Christmas- Luther Vandross

5. Eight Days Of Christmas- Destiny's Child

6. Sweet Love- Anita Baker

7. Bring Me Love- John Legend

8. Nothing Can Change This Love- Sam Cooke

9. White Christmas- Babyface

1
GENESIS

I wanted her.
God, I wanted her.
I wanted to coil her bouncy well-maintained curls around my greedy fingers, the ones she was careful to keep under her ever-changing rotation of wigs. I wanted to caress her impossibly soft umber skin, the same skin I watched glow under the Los Angeles sun every Monday. I wanted to kiss her perfect lips, and peck her cute wide nose, and I wanted her to look at me with those low-lidded puma eyes while she was wrapped in my fresh sheets. I wanted her so bad that it hurt if I thought about it too long.
Literally, because a lot of these slacks didn't have enough stretch in the crotch.

I've wanted her every day for the last seven years, and in a perfect world, she'd know that for as long as she lived. Anybody else would've made their move six years and

four months ago and maybe by then the magic of Brittany Barnes would've long worn off. I probably would've made my move too except by now she'd be my wife and I'd be cleaning her car every Monday and serving her breakfast in bed every Sunday. She seemed like she appreciated lazy Sundays and a good slice of strawberry French toast.
But there was just one problem:
She was my boss.

Brittany Barnes was the COO of Solei and I've worked in HR for the last seven or so years. She wasn't always the COO, but she should have been. Luckily the company got acquired by a New York venture capitalist named Marvin Rosenbloom, and after he fired approximately half the staff between here and Rosencorp, he personally appointed Black women in the positions left behind. I've long-learned not to applaud white men for taking a step in the right direction with their power, but he seems like a good one. Because Brittany had been killing it ever since. Sales are doing fantastic, engagement has sky-rocketed, and while most of the economy feels like it's at a stand-still, we've had unprecedented company growth. And it's all thanks to the 5'9 brown-skinned beauty who runs a tight ship. Which only made me want her more.

Now I know what you're thinking: "Dimitris, why don't you just leave that woman alone if she's doing so well?" Believe me, I've tried. Sometimes I stare at her so much that I creep myself out. Then I tell myself that I'm definitely going to get over her, that this will be the day.
But it never works.
As soon as I see her lick that airy mocha-tinged whipped cream off her glossy full lips during our Monday

catch-ups, I fold. It's a tragic cycle and it probably won't ever end, and that's why I'm going to do something about it in one week, five days, 4 hours, two minutes and 45 seconds. During our company Holiday Party.
I'm going to make Brittany Barnes mine.

Brit

The taste of peppermint and chocolate settled into my tongue like a warm hug, almost like an invisible blanket. It had perfectly coiffed whipped cream, a generous amount of chocolate sprinkles, and the ever-satisfying bite of full body dark roast coffee.
It was perfect, and so was the morning.
But I was wary.
Because someone was plotting on me, and I could feel it in the crisp LA winter air.

Don't get me wrong, that isn't anything new. Ya girl been that bitch and she's always gonna be that bitch. Plotting is just an unfortunate side effect. I've been plotted against since I was eight years old and won class president against Stephanie Andrews. She still makes "jokes" about the votes being miscounted.
But this doesn't feel like that. This feels different in a new way.
"Hey, Boss!" Sam cheered with a wave.
"Sam I Am, Brittany is preferred," I corrected gently.

Sam was a second year intern and my current PA. If we're being completely honest, my best PA. She scheduled, recommended, and reminded me to death, but she was probably the only reason I remembered to take my vitamins on time. She's made herself a huge part of my life and unfortunately, this was her last year with me according to the company.

But we'd see about that.

"Sorry, Brit. Ma spent the weekend bullying me about my 'Lack of respect in the office' since she saw us gossiping on Friday," Sam explained.

"You know she's just mad we didn't include her in it," I laughed, thinking of Sam's mom. "How is Ajumma anyway?"

"Nosey, but she sends kimchi and gochujang," Sam says, slipping the tape-marked Tupperware containers into my fridge.

My mouth watered instantly. Kimchi reminded me that I had a little brown rice and bulgogi chicken left, and I was happy daydreaming about that until Sam broke my food trance.

"She also says I need to do a better job as your assistant so you have extra time to find a nice boy."

I can't stop myself from rolling my eyes. Mrs. Heo is always hoping I meet a nice boy. She meant well but I'm not exactly sure how to break it to her that I'm living my best hoe life right now. Besides, in this dating market, I am the nice boy.

"Why can't a nice boy find me?" I groaned. "I'm tired of this, Grandpa!"

Sam was sorting through mail, but she doesn't miss a beat in her reply,

"Because boys don't come in nice. They come in irritating, tolerable, and decent."

Yikes.

And here I thought I was jaded when it came to love.

I don't bother containing my grimace as I spin to face her. Sam has recently been anti-man after a string of horrible dates and I can't say she's wrong, but part of me is crushed because I'm still holding out hope. Hope that prince charming is out there, waiting for me.

"I mean, someone had to have raised their son with some kind of sense," I sighed.

"Meh, I wouldn't count on it," Sam shrugged while starting the shredder. "The last one asked if I could add him to my credit card."

I nearly spat out my coffee remembering the soft-eyed blonde Sam showed me the last go around. According to his Vybe profile he was an engineer and a Stanford grad.

"On the first date!?" I shrieked. "I thought that one had money?"

"Oh, I forgot to tell you. He was an *audio* engineer," Sam laughed.

"God, another SoundCloud producer?"

"Yep, and his lo-fi sucked ass. My nephew makes better beats on his leap pad."

A throaty snort escaped me, and even though I swore it was just me and Sam, I felt like someone else was there watching me.

"You good, Brit?" Sam asked, as my head whipped around the room.

"Yeah, I'm ok," I replied while forcing my gaze from the strategically placed mirrors.

A tell-tale shiver raced down my spine the second those words left my lips. Something was off.

"Actually, I lied. Have you heard anything recently?"

"I mean, Samson is definitely cheating on his wife with Margie, Chris from the cafeteria has a drinking problem, and I'm like 80% sure the former CEO is headed to prison," Sam answered.

I said a silent prayer that I never fell out of Sam's grace because she really missed her calling as a PI. It's concerning that one little woman contains so much information. Concerning, yet commendable.

"That's informative yet kind of irrelevant," I mumbled. "I meant have you heard anything about me? Have I pissed anyone off?"

"Hm, let me think," Sam said, tapping her chin. "Besides Vanna Henry when you wear that extra snug navy sweater dress, no. Why do you ask?"

Mischief shone bright in her youthful brown eyes, yet so did truth. If anything was going on, Sam would know. She read people better than Iyanla Vanzant.

"No reason. I guess I've been a little paranoid lately," I chuckled. "I've been feeling like I'm being plotted on."

I felt silly finally saying that out loud to another person. So silly that my snort returned. I expected Sam's chuckle to join mine, but it never did. Instead she looked mortified.

"What?" I asked, swallowing my laughter.

"You need to listen to your gut, Brit," Sam said gravely. "Women's intuition is hardly ever wrong."

It was weird.

I wanted to wave her off, assure her that it was just my nerves and that there was nothing to worry about, but

I couldn't. Because that nagging feeling had returned again.
Someone was definitely watching me.

Dimitrius

I understand why women pick the bear.
Because men are fucking creepy, myself included. I was sitting in the fourth floor break room with my decoy snack while balancing my bulky-ass laptop on my knees. Not because I was hungry and unable to wait for lunch, no. But so I could watch Brittany's office from a safe distance.

This break room offered the perfect view of her desk, even when she had her shades drawn. Ironically, I discovered this completely by accident. Margie from culinary had subtly hinted that there would be brownies available in the fourth floor kitchen one day when my mood was particularly foul, and while waiting, I noticed Brittany pacing the length of her office, handling a phone call.

I remember the day perfectly. It was late spring but the temperature was officially summer. She had on a shift dress that stopped just above her knee and it matched the color of the plum orchard on her desk. Her hair was pulled into a low chignon, one that allowed me to see the sheen of the soft natural curls located at her nape. Her long brown legs strutted across the low carpet with precision, one in front of the other, switching off her weight and blessing me with the slight jiggle and sway of her carefully wrapped curves.

Margie sat the tray of brownies on the counter with a coy smile and they smelled heavenly, but I couldn't care less. My mouth was watering for something even richer. Something even sweeter.

That was the day I officially gave up trying to abandon my crush and embraced my obsession.

Because that's exactly what it was.

"Hey, Dimi. Are you going to catch-up?" a bubbly voice asked, breaking me from my Brit-watching.

I looked up into the eager eyes of Asali from under-writing, who awaited my response. Listen, I'm not stupid. Even without my four-year psychology program and subsequent two-year ABA, I know how to read people. Asali's flush face, inviting body language, and wide eyes hid nothing. I knew she had a crush on me. She's had a crush on me since I dropped her new hire folder on her desk. However, I also knew that I had a unique advantage as head of HR, and that is the gift of elective ignorance. She would never tell me about her feelings directly because of my position, and I would never acknowledge it either. Don't get me wrong, Asali's beautiful, but she's not my type. She's a church mouse and I like sassy, demanding pussycats. Plus I'm a bad Muslim and she's devout. I enjoy pepperoni pizza and BLTs a little too much.

"Yes, I'm just finishing my uh," I started before recalling what I was supposed to be snacking on. "My s'mores Poptart."

Honestly, I don't like s'mores like that and I grabbed it just to blend in, but these little things are surprisingly good, especially when microwaved.

"Oh," she replied in a cool voice. "Wait, doesn't that have gelatin in it?"

"Probably," I nodded while stuffing the rest of the treat into my mouth. "But what my Baba doesn't know won't hurt him."

"Yes, but what about Allah? He will know."

Speaking of the man in charge, I said a silent prayer thanking him for my poker face. I get irritated almost every second of every day and no one ever knows, and they're not going to either.

"Ah, you're right," I conceded to Asali with a chuckle. "But please excuse me, I need to wash my hands."

I gathered my belongings, having absolutely no intention of returning but Asali interrupted me by gently tugging the sleeve of my shirt. Annoyance rose in my spirit seeing her hand clinging to my once wrinkle-free cotton button down because I don't like to be touched at work. It's intimate in my opinion, and work is not the place for intimacy.

I know that's a strange take considering my huge crush on Brittany and American business culture, but my mama taught me early on that co-workers aren't the same thing as friends. Asali is and will always be strictly a coworker. We don't know each other outside of here. Because if we did she would know better than to grab my shirt and it wouldn't take me staring her down for the better part of a minute for her to remove her hand.

"Actually, I can wait for you and we can walk down to the conference rooms together," she offered timidly.

Yikes, I ain't know about all that.

My mind raced trying to find the best response to shut that down without being an asshole about it, but luckily God was on my side. In walked Saeed from IT, just the guy I was hoping to run into.

"Asali, have you met Saeed?" I asked, pulling him into the conversation.

He had a ripe banana in his hand that I'm sure he intended to scarf down before the meeting, but he could save that for later. I needed him to focus on now. Smile and wave, pretty boy. Smile and wave.

"No, I don't think I have," Asali smiled.

Saeed played his part perfectly. He willowed over her, smiled brightly, and offered her his hand without any additional queues. Tall, handsome, and a slight himbo, I knew he'd be her cup of tea months ago during his new hire orientation.

"Well, Saeed here works in IT. He handles hardware repairs, but he's currently trying to move to underwriting. I think you two also go to the same Mosque. Why don't you accompany him to the meeting and catch him up on what's happening over there?"

There.

The seed was sowed, and now all Asali had to do was water it. God, I hoped she watered it. I was about to pass out waiting for her coy little smile, but it crept onto her face with surety.

"That sounds nice," she replied with a nod.

I did an internal air pump while patting Saeed on the shoulder. He'd never know it, but he saved me one very awkward conversation. Plus I'd be meaning to do this anyway. It's just hard to catch them at the same time.

What do I mean, you ask?

Well lots of men have physical hobbies like basketball, woodworking, or even vehicle restoration if they're especially talented. My hobby, however, is match making. I've quietly orchestrated five marriages, two engagements, and six long-term relationships, and something about the dizzy smile Asali gave Saeed as they walked down the hall together told me this would be number seven. Which was perfect because it gave me plenty of time to work on number eight: Me and Brittany.

2 PLANNERS

Brittany

I won't lie, I secretly hated Monday Morning catch-ups. I know they're essential to the business since we had adaptive scheduling and most people were out of the office by the afternoon, but I am not a morning person. It disturbs my spirit to have to open my mouth and sustain a conversation before 9am and I'm usually the lead on these things. The only good thing about catch-ups is the very brief amount of time I got to spend looking at Dimi's fine ass. He was a short king through and through at just 5"6, but God gave with both hands when it came to his face card. His pearly, dimpled smile was highly lickable. He had the smoothest skin that was reminiscent of cured henna, and deep brown eyes that reminded me of recently unearthed truffles.

We'd grown close over the years with our coffee breaks, shared lunches, and little inside jokes and sometimes that made me wonder what more than work friends could look like. But unfortunately Dimitrius was the head of Human Resources and everyone with sense knows you can't flirt with HR.
That's like flirting with the unemployment line directly.
Oh, well though.
He was still fun to look at. Especially when he wore that ruby sweater with the elbow patches over his button downs. I'll take heart stopping rides for $500, Alex.

Today was no different. He strode in quickly, dressed in a pair of dark gray slacks and a navy blue button down. Dimi had been wearing a lot of blue lately. Almost like he knew it was my favorite color. I mean, I knew that was unlikely but I was appreciative regardless. It put some pep in my step.

As soon as he sat down in the chair across from mine , the crowd finished trickling in. He gave me a small smile that silently encouraged me and then his undivided attention. So I rose from the table and got to work.
"Good morning, everyone!" I said brightly. "We're at the end of the year. So let's get this show on the road so everybody can get back to what's really important. Holiday plans."
The room laughed at Dimi's charge, and I noticed a twinkle in his eye. Something optimistic told me that would be the best catch-up yet.

Update:
It was the worst catch-up yet. Miranda from Committees

And Planning had taken an early maternity leave, and no one had the foresight to ask her what we still needed to do for the annual company holiday bash before she left. A few in attendance suggested calling her, but I was friends with Miranda in real life and I had the absolute honor of seeing photos of her chunky, adorable, new-born daughter, so I shut that down fast. Thus knighting myself as the default planner for the festivities.
Yay me.

The crowd filed out quickly while I stayed behind to type a few notes. I only noticed I wasn't alone after I heard chairs being pushed back in.
"Hey, Brittany. It was nice of you to take over for Miranda," Dimitrius said, helping me collect my scattered things.
"It's fine," I replied with a shrug. "She deserves to spend this time with her baby. She's a one-woman superband."
"That she is," he laughed. "But you don't have to be."
My head snapped around like a thin switch in the wind at his statement.
"What do you mean?" I asked.
Dimitrius shrugged, showing off those nice broad shoulders of his.
"I mean exactly that. You don't have to do this alone. I'll be your co-captain in this. I know you already have a lot on your plate with the upcoming New Year and I want to help," he explained.

My hand flew to my chest to calm my racing heart. All jokes aside, I really did like my job. But this man was making me rethink everything. Even though I swore I wouldn't bother him.
"Ok, I'd like that," I said quietly.

Too quietly if we're being honest.

It kind of scared me how quick I softened toward him, and once I noticed he was affecting me, I immediately straightened my back. If Dimitrius noticed, he didn't say anything. He just gave me a respectable coworker smile and passed me his business card.

"Great! Of course you can find me on Slack, but here's all the ways you can reach me. If you want, I can put a meeting on your calendar for Friday and we can come up with a plan of action and start dividing our tasks," he offered cheerfully.

I keep a revolving mental checklist of qualities I look for in a partner. Not because I'm actively searching for a long-term relationship, but so I don't accidentally pass on a good thing just because of a good time. Dimi was so very off-limits, but damn if he wasn't everything I wanted and more.

Emotionally intelligent? Check. Considerate? Check. Kind? Check. Take-charge in a way that made me want to turn my brain off and hand over my panties, no questions asked? Double check.

What I'm trying to say is, he was dangerous.

And my goofy behind liked it.

"O-ok," I stammered. "I'll be looking out."

"Good. Well. I'll see you then!" Dimi said, extending his hand.

I don't prefer handshakes, but I understand they're commonplace in the corporate world. Something about Dimi offering me his hand felt different though. His grip was strong but still gentle. His palms were warm, and his skin was buttery soft. He held my gaze the entire time we touched. It reminded me of holding hands with a crush for the first time, which probably would've scared me if my sense hadn't plummeted to my pussy. But truthfully I didn't mind it.

Until it was time to let go.

"See you around, Brit," Dimi said with a heavy amount of lingering eye contact.

"Yeah, see you," I waved with my heart still hammering against my ribs,

Dimitrius

Brittany's favorite color is blue.

I know that because she mentioned it once during a lead icebreaker, five years ago. In that same vein, she also mentioned that her favorite season was Winter because of all the holiday drinks, specifically peppermint mochas. Which is exactly what I brought to our meeting on Friday. This holiday party collab was not a part of my original plan, but damn it if I didn't make wooing her much easier.

I gently tapped on her door, making sure not to bang on her shit like the police. Because she was one of those black women who didn't like unnecessary noise. Not that I could blame her. I hated the sound of lawn mowers and box fans.

Five seconds after my tap, her assistant answered.

"Hi, Sam," I said cheerfully. "I have a meeting with Brittany."

One thing about Sam, she's efficient. So efficient that she has notes for her notes. I've never seen anything go wrong since Sam became Brittany's assistant, and if I know Brittany, which I do, then I knew she was going to figure out a way to get Sam to stay long-term. What I didn't know, however, was how Sam was going to affect my little scheme. To be completely honest, I forgot to account for her. That was a researcher error.

She didn't let me in, she just zeroed her focus on the drink carrier I was holding.

"What's in the cup?" she asked, almost accusingly.

Her voice had a hard edge that dared me to lie. You'd think I was carrying poison the way she acted. That was alright though, I didn't pale in the face of a challenge.

"A peppermint mocha."

"It's ten. She doesn't drink caffeine after ten."

"I know," I nodded. "It's decaf."

"You know?" she responded with a glare. "That's interesting."

She stared at me, her slanted brown eyes trying to break me down and make me confess, but I was the king of interrogations. There was a reason I was so good at match-making and my actual day job. I was the master of emotional control.

"And what's the meeting about?" she asked, still glaring.

"The holiday party."

"Really? Nothing else?" she followed up. "No other kinds of planning?"

"Not at the moment," I smiled while rocking on my heels. "But I'll be sure to let you know if that changes."

She scoffed at me like I was common scum. I don't know what I did to get on Sam's infamous shit list, but I wondered how much longer we'd have to do this considering Brittany's drink was getting cold. However, after hearing the woman of the hour exit the bathroom, Sam begrudgingly stepped aside.

"Dimitrius is here for your ten, Boss Lady," she announced. "I'll be at my desk if you need me."

"Alrighty!" Brittany replied. "Take a breakfast break, Sam. We don't have anything else going on until twelve."

"If you say so," Sam said, still side-eyeing me. "Call me if you need me, Brit."

"Thank you!" I exclaimed.

"Dimitrius," she gritted, closing the door.

"What was that about?" Brittany asked.

"I have no idea," I shrugged, having a general idea. "Peppermint mocha?"

"Oh, yes!" she shrieked while sliding her drink out of the cardboard carrier. "Wait."

"Don't worry, it's decaf," I said with a smile. "I wouldn't wanna give you the jitters."

"Mr. Karimi, you shouldn't have," she giggled. "Thank you."

I definitely, definitely should always. Especially if you keep saying my name like that.

"I also grabbed you a pistachio croissant."

I slid the treat across the desk and Brittany's pupils blew wide, like she was taking a hit of something potent. She almost threw her drink down trying to get to that croissant. I knew my Instagram stalking would come in handy.

"Ohmygod," she garbled while taking a bite. "I haven't had one of these in almost a year. I forgot how good they are."

"They're one of my favorites too," I said, unwrapping my

own pastry.

I took a bite and let the smooth pistachio cream settle onto my tongue. My mouth watered instantly, and then I locked gazes with Brittany, who was making this experience unexpectedly erotic for me. Don't get me wrong, Dough Boy's pastries were good, but not that good. Still Brittany's low-lidded eyes tracked my every bite. She licked the leftover filling off her lips with a gentle sweeping motion that made my overactive imagination run like a wild stallion. Then to make matters worse, her chest heaved with the softest pleased moan. It rang in my ears like a siren, calling me to action. I sat up in my chair, trying to hide the evidence that my body was ready and waiting.

"So about the holiday party," Brittany sighed.
"What about it?" I asked absentmindedly, my attention lingering on her lips.
God, she had nice lips. Lips that looked good enough to eat.
"I went over the notes and it looks like we still need to handle catering and decorations. Everything else is in order."
Oh right. We were in fact planning a holiday party.
"Which would you prefer handling?" I asked.

Brittany's desk was adorned in glittering tinsel, strings of tiny ornaments, and vibrant flickering lights all set against a red velvet tablecloth. So I already knew she'd want decorations over catering and I didn't mind one bit. Still I held off on taking it over until she gave me her say-so. I wanted to show her that her preferences were my priority.

"To be completely honest, I hate dealing with catering," she admitted.

"Say no more. You handle decorations, and I got catering. I was looking at a few possibles earlier just in case. I sent the list to you in an email."

Brittany spun towards her computer with a strange look on her face, and once she clicked the email to confirm that look transformed into an impressed smile.

"Wow, is this organized by cuisine and price?" she asked, scrolling through my document.

"Yes, and also star rating," I replied.

Brittany tapped her fingers against her desktop, her short almond nails making a little tune as she skimmed the document.

"Dimi this is amazing," she cooed.

"And so are you." I thought quietly. *"So are you."*

"I'm really liking the first two. It's just something about a macaroni bar in the winter," Brittany said after a while.

I figured as much. While most Californians trembled in the face of carbs, Brittany rejoiced in them. She loved bread, pasta, rice, and potatoes.

"I agree. Who doesn't want cheesy noodles loaded up with bacon, green onion, and barbeque sauce?"

"Wait, is that your favorite combination?" she gasped.

"Yeah," I sighed. "I know the barbecue sauce sounds we-"

"No no!" Brittany interjected. "That's exactly how I eat mine. Sometimes I'll even throw some chopped brisket or grilled chicken in there if I'm feeling fancy."

My stomach growled as I pictured the perfect bowl of Mac and cheese in my mind. Gooey, hot, and covered in meat. I started to crave it even though I never thought of it prior to thirty seconds ago.

"Ooh, I've never had it like that," I said, rubbing my chin. "Baked or stovetop?"

"Baked of course," she giggled while twirling a strand of hair around her pointer finger. "With crushed up fried onions instead of breadcrumbs."

Damn, she was a professional.

"Marry me?" I replied while sliding my hand down my face.

She laughed but I wasn't joking. A nigga was dead serious. I even had the plot of land we were going to build our dream house on picked out. Excellent school district, close to a shopping center, but still safe with low traffic.

"We can do a macaroni swap once all this party stuff settles," she suggested with a nervous smile. "I owe you some food anyway for the harira."

We could do way more than just swap macaroni. We could produce a whole macaroni playlist if she was in the mood.

These were insane thoughts for a Tuesday afternoon meeting, I know. But everything about Brittany hypnotized me and sent me somewhere else. Her style, her humor, her love of carbs. The way the left corner of her mouth just barely ticked up when she was trying to withhold a smile.

Her existence.

"Dimi, is that ok?" she asked, softly touching my hand.

"More than ok," I replied excitedly while placing my hand

over hers.

She did it again.

The left corner of her mouth twitched from the pressure of a barely contained smile. She let go of my hands and her eyes whipped down to focus on a stray piece of fuzz on her tablecloth, but it was too late. I had already seen that little smirk. Now I was making it my mission to see her actually laugh.

Something I wanted so desperately it hurt.

Yeah, Brittany Barnes was going to be my wife.

"You're plotting on my boss and I'm filing a lawsuit with the EEOC if you don't confess right now!" Sam shrieked. Turns out not accounting for Sam was a major misstep on my part. Because her observant ass was about to tank my plan on step 1.

"Sam, relax. I can explain," I said, holding my hands up. She had cornered me in the garage elevator with a stapler. While it wasn't the best weapon, it was a weapon nonetheless. Especially for clothes. I couldn't risk my jacket. It was one of my clearance treasures.

"Get to explaining then, Coffee Boy!" she hollered, aiming the stapler towards my palm.

Yeah, I smacked that shit out of her hand. I didn't have time to even play like that.

"Now since that's settled, here's the truth. I am plotting on Brittany…"

"I knew it!" she shrieked, uncapping her pen and revealing a microphone. "Say goodbye to your pension, fuck face."

"ROMANTICALLY SPEAKING!" I shouted in a hurry.

Sam's victorious grin fell before slowly creeping back into a weird smile. She tapped a little button on her pen before slipping it back into her bag. That thing was deceptively full. I also spotted a soup canister and a knife among its contents.

"Wait, you like Brittany?"

"Yes," I nodded.

"So do you like-like her or are you just trying to smash?"

"Nope, we're not doing that," I said firmly.

Was I trying to fuck Brittany? Yes, of course. Was that the only reason I was obsessed with the ground she walked on? No, not even close.

"Ok, that's fair. But why are you being weird about it?" Sam asked.

"Um," I said, momentarily looking at my feet to gather my thoughts.

My mind flashed back to the first day we met. She was an intern herself, and I was the new kid on the block. It was my first day of my official big boy job. Don't get me wrong, I had been working years prior but I never had benefits, vacation time, or an office. So I was nervous. Mostly because I had more to lose.

Brittany saw me fidgeting in the elevator and instead of

ignoring me and focusing on her own task, she gave me a soft smile.

"You're going to do great. Your brain doesn't know what it's talking about," she laughed.

I wanted to agree but my racing thoughts were busy telling me otherwise. So many things had the potential to go wrong. I had people's livelihood in my hands.

"But what if…"

"What ifs don't exist today. Just do your best. That's all you can do." Her words hit me in the chest, instantly soothing my anxiety, and I returned her gorgeous smile. Then she swung her drink carrier around and handed me her cup. *"I usually get a ginger chamomile tea. They help me relax. Here try it."*

Honestly, I didn't like tea. Coffee was my blood type at that point in my life. But for some reason I took it. Our fingers brushed as she passed me the paper cup, sending heat dancing across my skin. I brought the warm drink to my mouth and took a few sips in an effort to explain my obvious blushing. Then the strangest thing happened. I relaxed. The tension bled from my shoulders immediately.

"See? I told you," she smiled, blocking out the sound of the elevator ding. *"Oh, this is my floor. See you around!"*

She got off with her lead's coffee and my heart in her pocket and I hadn't been the same since. Not even my day-to-day recovered.

I prefer my ginger chamomile with honey and lemon now, and I drink it daily.

"I really want this to work out," I sighed, scratching the back of my head. "I **need** this to work out."

"Oh, you like her for real," Sam laughed when spotting my expression. "Ok. I'm in. How can I help?"

My flabbers were gasted. 15 seconds before, I thought the only way I'd leave this garage was with a knife wound. Now Sam was offering her help?

"Wait what? I thought you hated men?" I exclaimed.

Brittany Barnes' PA had a reputation. I tried not to believe in rumors and heresy, but Sam was a certified man eater. She broke a heart a week. It bumped up to two during the summer.

"I don't hate men," she scoffed. "I just think they're generally useless. But you seem different, and Brit needs different."

Different. I desperately wanted to give her something different. Something endearing. Something only meant for her.

"Alright, lover boy. Knock those stars out of your eyes and tell me the plan," Sam said with a wave. "I'm ready to go home."

After watching Brittany devour that croissant, I too wanted to go home. Home to a nice cold shower. So I detached from my daydream with nervous laughter and gave Sam the rundown,

"So this is what I was thinking..."

Brittany

"Holy shit," I whispered.

We were getting down to the wire when it came to the Christmas party. Dimi had handled the catering and bar situation as promised, but I was catching hell when it came to decorations. The original vendor had double booked us with a wedding so the crystal chiavari chairs I wanted were no longer available. They offered us black Montgomery brawl chairs instead. While that would've been fine for something like a picnic, the company holiday party was high stakes. So that left me twelve days to find a vendor who could work with us, on top of managing shipments, party favors, and entertainment stations on top of my regular workload. Needless to say, ya girl was stressed.

I needed a pick-me-up and I had fully planned on getting one after work, but when I walked in my office, I saw **it.**
"Sam, where the fuck did this come from?" I exclaimed.
Sitting on my desk in all its glory, was a Hoya Lauterbachii. It was big and beautiful, with bright blooms, green leaves, and a stunning, seemingly handmade copper and clay pot.
"I think it's from a secret admirer," Sam said in a sickly sweet tone. "Here's the card."
I snatched up the card, hoping it offered some clue as to who left a $250 plant on my desk, but alas it just said,
"A *plant befitting a rare beauty such as yourself. Happy first day of Christmas.*"
No name, no clues, no nothing.

"And you didn't see who dropped it off?" I asked Sam.
She gave me a lazy shrug while arranging the pot,
"Nope, it was here when I got in."
I didn't believe that for one second. Sam often beat out the facility folks in the morning. I once caught her shooting dice with one of the overnight janitors who she had

convinced to stay past his shift end. How she missed a whole-ass reverse burglar when she brewed coffee before culinary could, I don't know.

"As many times as I've told you to stop coming in so early and this is the one time you listen? Wow," I chuckled.
My eyes returned to the pot, and I noticed my initials were carved into the luxurious pottery. This plant had been on my wish list for years and I've never been lucky enough to catch one. I didn't like surprises, but I had to admit this was a good one. Good and thoughtful. Some real Rom-Com level shit.
"As long as they're cute, I guess there's no harm in this one thing," I sighed in defeat.
"Exactly!" Sam exclaimed with a clap. "No harm at all."
Right. No harm at all. I just needed my anxiety-filled belly to get the memo...

"Wow, nice wax plant," Dimi mumbled.
I looked up from my stack of advertising contracts, right into the head of HR's waiting brown eyes.
God, that man was fine.
I didn't even think they made them like that anymore but there he was with a broad, dazzling smile, a jaw carved out of a mountainside to match, and the most beckon-

ing gaze I've ever seen in my life. Now that's someone I wouldn't mind getting secret gifts from. But alas, I knew that wasn't a possibility. Dimi was very professional. He kept it cute and friendly, but nothing more.

"Yeah, somebody broke into my office this morning and left it here," I said, peeking at the pretty pot once more.
"Broke in?" Dimi queried with raised brows.
"Well not literally," I replied with a wave. "But somehow they got past Sam, so maybe."
"Well alright," Dimi said cautiously, taking a seat across from me. "Anyway, I stopped by to talk about the chairs."
"Ugh, please don't remind me," I groaned.
I never thought that securing rental chairs would be this difficult. With just barely two weeks to go and a busy holiday season, it was impossible to find vendors who weren't already booked. Plus the ones that weren't booked had raggedy ass chairs with gangsta leans. I wasn't handing someone $2,500 to potentially fall on my ass during dinner.

"No, no, don't worry. I have good news," Dimi smiled. "I called in a favor with a friend and we'll be able to get the crystal chiavari chairs you wanted originally. At half the price."
I just barely resisted the urge to jump out of my chair and kiss Dimitrius on the mouth.
"How?" I shrieked.
"Like I said, I called in a favor. I couldn't have us potentially hosting the LA chapter of the waterside brawl."
I snorted before I could realize it, then I threw my hand over my mouth to cover the source of such an ugly sound. Damn Dimitrius Karimi for making me genuinely laugh! I

hadn't done that at work in years. He really was dangerous.

"So that's what you sound like without that wall," Dimitrius said with eyes full of wonder. "It suits you."
"Thank you," I whispered while uncovering my mouth.
Wait, did he just say he liked my laugh?
My cheeks tingled from the rush of hot blood. My thumping heart was busy reminding me that I was alive while my
brain launched into code red. The words, **UNEMPLOY-
MENT**, flashed big and bold in my mind. But unfortunately that didn't stop the butterflies from fluttering in my
tummy. Everything around me was devolving into classic
end of the year chaos, and while I never truly could tell
what was happening, I knew for sure that I was starting to
develop a crush on Dimitrius Karimi. Human Resources
long-standing department head.
This was a problem.

"Well, anyway. I'll let you get back to it," Dimi said, tapping
on the desk.
He stood slowly, giving me time to drag my gaze across
his firm body, and I did so shamelessly. Yes, I knew that he
could see me, but laughing during business hours for the
first time in years had me throwing caution to the wind.
Indulging in a few looks was fine as long as I kept my
degenerate thoughts to myself. Which was no problem
because I'd definitely have to take some of my fantasies
to the grave. Especially the ones involving Dimi and that
gold buckle brown leather belt he loved so much.

"Alright," I managed to say with some semblance of nor-
malcy. "And thank you again for the chairs. I owe you

one."

Dimitrius pauses his stride and turns to face me with an expression that can only be described as keen.

"You don't owe me, Brit," he said firmly. "I'd do nearly anything just to enjoy the privilege of your presence."

Jesus Devonte Christ!

Everyone knows LA is hot but the way my very off-limits coworker looked at me turned my body molten. If I didn't get it together soon, janitorial was going to have to mop me up off the floor. So I swallowed the lump in my throat, which was probably my heart, and nodded.

"Ok," I replied in a small voice.

I then watched his lips dip into a slight smile as he walked through the door and afterwards I silently screamed in my seat.

Fuck, I was in trouble.

3
One In The Hand

I don't know about twelve days.

She's already skeptical.

I know. I'll probably call in a favor with Kane in facilities and Jacie in the mail room. That way they just arrive at random times throughout the day.

Sounds good. I'll get him a key.

Oh, and Dimitrius?

Hm?

Don't fuck this up, lover boy.

Dimitrius

I'm rarely wrong, but rarely doesn't mean never.
I thought I might have been wrong about this thing with Brittany being mutual for a brief second, but then she looked at me like I was walking sex because I secured chairs. I'm stupid though because I almost blew my cover on day one saying what I said about her presence, but a nigga has his limits. Desire can only fester quietly for so long. Any later and I might have been sweating it out. Especially since she came to work in a plaid mini skirt and a pair of reindeer antlers the next day.
She could definitely guide my sleigh tonight, tomorrow, and forever.

"Oh my God!" Brittany exclaimed.
I smiled into my coffee mug from the safety of the fourth floor break room. Day two was off to a great start. In recent years, I've learned that Brit is essentially a cat. Nocturnal, sassy, and a seeker of cozy. She loved a nice throw, especially in cooler months. And you could often find them slung over the back of her desk chair in a neat square or spread over her lap. I went with the former option and left her second gift folded in pleats to display the knitted pattern.
"Is this cashmere!?" she shrieked
"Looks like Merino wool," Sam replied cooly.
It was for sure Merino wool and Sam knew it. As previously displayed, we had to rework our plan after yesterday's near disaster. Brittany was way too smart for us to be playing with her like that. So today I snuck in while they

were at lunch and left her gift, a blue and white two person Moroccan throw embroidered with gray turtle doves.

"How much does something like this even cost?" I heard Brittany ask.

She'd never know it, but the answer was a lot and that's even with the generous discount my Khala gave me. However, that didn't matter. What mattered was the brief look of contentment that flashed across her face when she finally picked it up. Until she said,

"I think I need to call the police. I must have a stalker."

Shit!

That was not the reaction I hoped to invoke. What was I going to do now?

"You definitely do not have a stalker, Boss Lady," Sam replied.

"Ion know, this is too spot on. It's in my favorite color and everything. How else would you explain it?"

"Maybe it's a friend shooting their shot," Sam shrugged.

Brittany turned towards Sam with gaze full of regret and sincerity.

"Sam, I love you, but–"

"Not me, damnit! I'm not balling like that!" Sam shrieked. "A different friend."

"Oh, well what other friends do I have here?" Brittany queried.

Ouch that hurt, but I also understood. HR wasn't exactly a glamorous job and it definitely didn't contribute to the growth of long standing employee friendships. Everyone saw HR as the employment grim reaper and normally that didn't bother me, but I hoped our years together could change her mind.

"You literally have friends everywhere," Sam scoffed. "Your butcher is in your book club."
"That's pure coincidence, I assure you," Brittany argued.
"Sure, Jan. Anyway, my point is that you have friends everywhere. And maybe one wants to be more than friends."
"God, Ajumma is getting to you," Brittany sighed before her eyes illuminated.
"Wait, do you know who it is?"
I choked on my coffee. My planning flashed right before my eyes. For everything I'd done right, I'd done one thing wrong. Me and Sam forgot to plan a decoy. I was cooked.
"No I do not," Sam said plainly and Brittany shot her a disbelieving look.
"Contrary to popular belief, I don't know everything. I still don't know who keeps taking my inkjoys."

It was Kevin from the concierge team. He was a fancy, cheap, asshole. He wore designer down to his socks only to "borrow" pens, coffee mugs, and headphones. Plus sanitation had a suspicion that even that cheap ass one ply toilet paper was on his snatch and grab list. The day his termination paperwork came across my desk I would jump for joy, but unfortunately today wasn't that day.
No.
Instead, today was the day I would find out what happened when you flew too close to the sun.

"Yeah, you're right," Brittany sighed, running a hand down her beautiful face. "The paranoia is getting to me."

I hated that we had to gaslight her, but HALLELUJAH! I was safe and it was all thanks to that little psychopath, Sam. When she agreed to help me, she made it clear in no uncertain terms that I'd owe her one, but so far she was worth every terrifying possibility I envisioned. In just ten more days, I was going to have my cake and eat Brittany's too.

I couldn't wait for Christmas.

Brittany

There were 17 days left of the year, and eight days left until my adult version of a winter vacation. I always took ten days off following the company holiday party to regroup and recharge which I desperately needed to do after the year I'd had. But there was just one problem.

The gifts.

So far I had received the wax plant, the throw, a custom self-heating mug, and a wallet that matched my favorite purse. The wallet was what really set it off, since they were now out of production and a very rare find on resale markets.

"Well?" I asked, motioning to my pile of gifts on the kitchen table.

"Well what?" Mama laughed while stirring her sauce. "It looks like somebody is kicking his goal."

"Shooting his shot, Beverly," Daddy corrected from his spot on the couch.

He was reviewing the household budget, which for some reason he preferred to do on paper, while my mama made dinner. Music surged through the soundbars, encouraging Mama to shimmy while Daddy occasionally sang

along to the smooth crooning of Sam Cooke and Bobby Womack, his happiness evident in every high note.
My parents really were the perfect pair.

"You know what I mean," she clicked back. "Some young man is interested."
"I never said it was a man," I argued.
"Ha. That's a man all day everyday. Look at that handwriting. He writes like a typewriter. David, come look!"
"Baby, I don't care about some man's handwriting. Sierra's book costs this semester are bleeding me dry," Daddy replied gruffly.
"Tuh, you the one who wanted all these smart babies. How does it feel now that you're three Master's degrees in?" Mama scoffed.
"Better now that Brittany has her man friend," Daddy chuckled.
Lawd.
"That's not what this is!" I protested.

I came to my parent's house straight from work, hoping they'd give me some actual advice. But instead they were cracking jokes.
Lots of jokes.
"What's he look like? Can he jump?" Mama asked, while sliding her cast iron into the oven.
Ever since my brother brought home a white woman Thanksgiving prior, they'd been holding their breath for us last two. Don't get me wrong, Chelsea is a sweetheart and really the best cast scenario. But her family?
Eh.

"It's turmeric on one of those cards so he's at least brown," Daddy replied.

His forensic investigator brain was still firing on all cylinders despite his now five year retirement, because I didn't even notice that.

"Thank God. I can't handle a Dianna Ross situation on my deathbed," Mama chuckled, her hazel eyes shimmering with amusement.

"Can y'all focus!?" I chided. "This is serious. I don't know who's leaving me these gifts. It's concerning!"

Whoever the culprit is was smart. I tried to follow the time pattern from the first two gifts, but they were inconsistent. The handwriting on the cards, as my mama pointed out, was oddly mechanical with no hint of personality. The gifts were very unique and I probably could've used that, but they were scraped clean of any tags or purchase indicators. I was either dealing with a serial killer or a perfectionist.

"Well what did Sammy say?' Mama asked.

I grumbled my reply, knowing exactly how this conversation would play out.

"She's not concerned."

"Oh well it's probably fine. You know she sniffs out bullshit better than a bloodhound."

"Yeah, but you know how I am. I don't like the unknown, and gifts from strangers are the unknown. I just want to figure this out, return the gifts, and start my vacation."

"Bullshit! Don't return nothing. A man wanna spend his money on you, you let him. Don't turn down nothing but your collar. I taught you better than that," Daddy griped with his Knoxville accent shining through.

"Daddy, the plant alone is like $200! What if I find out who it is and I'm not interested?"

"Then he gone have to charge it to the game. Besides, he clearly ain't hurting for money. That blanket alone is at least $400.

"How do you know that?" I gulped.

"Because there's a lady in my craft group who makes stuff just like that. The yarn cost is about a third of that."

My breath got caught in my throat. Don't get me wrong, I don't mind spending a lil money, but Jesus Christ on a cracker that's a lot of money for a blanket. A blanket that you gift someone else at that.

"Daddy, you worked for the police for forty years. How is this not concerning?" I pressed.

"Because if he hasn't tipped off Sam, but he knows you well enough to get you tailored gifts, he's probably safe. It's likely just an overlooked friend, in which case I ap-plaud his effort. It shows intent," Daddy explained while stapling his budget estimates. "I won't lie, I was con-cerned about your romantic prospects after that last boy you brought through here. You were a business major and he was a Lyric Boom rapper."

"SoundCloud, David," Mama interjected as she fixed plates.

"Tuh," he said, waving her off. "It don't matter what it was because he was a bum. I like this young man. He seems considerate."

Suddenly a lightbulb illuminated in my mind. I was look-ing for creeps when I needed to be looking for a consid-erate, Type-A, lover boy. I had the usual suspects. I'd been going about this all wrong.

"I know exactly what I'm going to do!" I shrieked.

"Sit down and eat dinner?" Mama asked. "The fish is getting cold."

Despite my newfound determination, a hot meal did sound nice. Especially my Mama's fish and spaghetti. And she made cornbread? I was sat.

"Yes that, but also I'm going to find this man. Before the end of the week."

"Ugh," my parents both groaned, likely frustrated with my tenacity.

"Goodness, you suck the fun out of everything," Daddy scoffed.

Well if it wasn't the pot calling the kettle black. I think back to all the times he picked apart the simplest things just to prove a

point and it made me smile.

"I get it from my Daddy," I replied.

Dimitrius

Brittany's father was in her office. He spoke to me this morning and asked if I could give pointers to Brittany's sister, Sierra, about our internships.

It's not the first time he's visited Brit at work, but something about his timing felt more than coincidental. Especially with him installing a camera on her desk. I was going to have to get creative with my gift giving now.

But camera aside, this was throwing a serious wrench in my plans. I was neurotic enough to plan out exactly how I was going to introduce myself to her parents. I'd wait until we got to six months, ask her how she felt like we we're doing, and then make the suggestion. We'd start with my parents first, mostly because they're simultaneously the easiest and the most awkward introduction. My mama would love her, undoubtedly. She'd do the traditional thing and ask Brittany to invite her parents to lunch so they could all meet. I'd woo them with a nice box of fruit and some wine to pair it with, and make my intentions known.

And this is the part where I realize I might be too far gone.

Maybe my Khala was right.

Maybe I did need to smoke some weed and relax.

"Hey, Dimi. Everything ok?" Brittany asked, snapping me out of my thoughts.

She stood before me in all her sun kissed beauty wearing a navy turtleneck, a khaki midi skirt, and a brown longline jacket. Her hair was up in a clip today, she'd gone with a cropped wig that framed her gorgeous high cheekbones, and she wore that signature mocha brown lipstick of hers. The one that made me realize I was staring only when she drew her lip between her teeth, waiting for my reply. That's when I also noticed I was pouring salt in my coffee instead of powdered creamer.

"Uh, yeah I'm fine," I grimaced before pouring my coffee down the sink. "Just a little stressed about my after-noon."

"I bet. I know accounting squeezed in some new hires before this quarter ended so they could start in January. That must be exhausting," she said.

It was, but honestly I hadn't given it much thought beyond her mentioning it. Simply because I was working towards a goal. I was working towards her. That was dangerous. Mostly because I had read enough psychology texts to know I suffered from tunnel vision. I just hoped it wasn't leading to my unknowing end.

"Yeah, a little. But it's ok. It's my job," I replied.

I watched mindlessly as Brittany scooped coffee grounds into the basket before filling the machine with water. She always moved with grace and elegance even when performing the most mundane tasks. She was like a fairy.

"I mean, yeah, it's your job. But that doesn't make your complaints any less valid. It's ok to be tired. That's what makes us human," she said.

My mind snapped back three years prior. To before Brittany officially became COO. At that point, she was doing the job without the title, and because that's what the former COO expected of her, she was ignoring her own needs. She came in sick as a dog one day, a combination of a cold and her period as she told me, and when I found out, I discharged her home with the harira I brought for lunch.

She was distraught. So distraught that she cried. She couldn't breathe through her nose but she still chose to use her precious air to inform me about deadlines, meetings, and other things that didn't really matter. That's when I told her,

"You're sick, and you're tired. And that's ok. It's ok to be tired. That's what makes us human. Go home and rest. If I see you back here before next Monday, I'll request a doctor's note."

She listened and went home. Stayed there for the rest of the week too. Then she came back in the following Monday, her normal Brittany self, with my washed container and a sweet thank you card.

"You remember that?" I asked.
"Yeah, of course," she shrugged. "I remember everything you say to me."
My mouth opened then promptly shut out of fear I'd find myself proposing to Brittany Barnes in the mud tracked fourth floor break room. She was waiting on a response but her hazel-eyed gaze had me preserved in a state of stillness, almost like a feather trapped in prehistoric amber.
She had rendered me speechless.
And I'm a certified yapper so that's hard to do.

"I-I should get going," I stammered, trying to shake the effects of her.
"Oh, um. I'm making coffee if you want to wait a little while. Since your first cup had to get dumped."
Her hands clasped against the front of her skirt and she nervously tangled her fingertips together while we maintained eye contact. So I stepped closer, hoping to ease her nerves. That soft bottom lip of hers was pinched between her teeth as she took a small step forward, meeting me in the middle. Our hands grazed just slightly before I carefully unraveled her hands and rubbed my thumb across her tight knuckles.

I couldn't stop the groan that escaped me when I once again realized how soft she was. It came from deep in my belly and flowed over my Adam's apple like a sacred hymn. I half-expected her to slap the shit out of me for being so forward, but instead her eyelids lowered from the sensation of our skin brushing. It amazed me that I got that reaction simply from my hand being on hers. There were no meetings on the fourth floor that day, and most employees had chosen to work from home for the last few weeks of the year. So it was just me and Brittany in that break room.

It was just us.

Whatever uncertainty I had about my pursuit being unwanted was thrown out of the window when she leaned slightly forward into my immediate air space. Dilated pupils, warm flushed skin, and oh-so inviting body language. Her lips parted like she wanted to tell me a secret that wasn't audible.

Brittany Barnes had a crush on me.

And I liked her too.

If she leaned any closer she was going to find out just how much.

Unfortunately the coffee machine beeped as coffee machines do when they're finished, and that ring pierced our quiet storm and reminded me to find my composure. While I was glad the feeling was mutual, truthfully, this was horrible timing. She'd be too worried about the end of the year and the upcoming party to enjoy anything between us. So against the wishes of every single screaming cell in my body, I said,

"I'll just take my coffee to go."

Brittany

I fucked up.

It happens sometimes though.

I thought me and Dimi, no *Dimitrius*, were sharing a moment for a second. He had this rapacious look in his eyes that told me we definitely were. But then something snapped in his brain when the coffee machine sounded and he peeled off like a spooked horse. Although I shouldn't really be surprised. There's a reason Dimitrius is the head of HR. He's understanding, but extremely logical. So I'm sure he had some internal risk-benefit analysis that determined the risk of kissing the COO wasn't worth it.

That was frustrating, but at least I could cross him off my list.

Sure he was sweet, considerate, and financially established, but my secret Santa had to be slightly brazen to risk creeping into my office, and Dimi wasn't that. He was the epitome of control. A perfect gentleman at all times. Which is kind of where I fucked up.

I came on to him.

Strong.

If anyone thought to run back those security tapes, there'd be no denying that I was about to suck that man's face. All I needed was a half a second to get my body in gear. I really do like my job, but it's something about Dimitrius that makes me forget my God-given sense. Maybe it was the smile that always pinches his eyes, or maybe it was simply due to his infectious laugh. It could've even been the fact that I could shoot him a look at any given time and he'd immediately understand. Even when it was that infamous, *I'm frustrated and they're pissing me off,* look. I'm not too sure what it was. But one thing I did know? If I ever got the chance, I was going to fuck the shit out of Dimitrius Karimi.

Dimitrius

"How's your plot going?"
A smile crept onto my face while I recalled Brittany's reaction to yesterday's gift and note. Day seven's gift was a classic cover of Vivid. There was a small shriek and an excited shimmy before she realized she'd been outdone and her new camera was essentially useless. Then she switched back to annoyed.
"Surprisingly well," I replied while sipping my bourbon.

Devin, my best friend, convinced me to go get drinks Saturday night so we could catch up. I usually decline public drinking for the sake of my parent's reputation and sanity, but he tempted me with habanero wings and a private speakeasy.
"So what's going to happen when you get to the end of all this and she realizes her prize is a half pint?" He teases.
"What's going to happen when this current girl of yours realizes that you stuff your left pants pockets with

socks?" I shot back.

Listen, I'm not insecure about my height. I'd made peace with the fact that I was slightly below average a long time ago. My Baba passed down plenty of other great qualities. My dimples, my brows, my shoulders, and my impeccable rhythm. It's just his love of short bossy women that conquered all.

"Aye bruh! It's not the size of the ship. It's the motion of the ocean!" he argued back.

"Whatever you say, pan fried shrimp," I shrugged. "That's y'all party. You can cry if you want to."

Devin pelted me with bar peanuts, but because I'm childish I started catching them in my mouth.

"You know for a nigga with an advanced psychology degree, you can be a real asshole at times. I thought you were supposed to understand when people were joking," he hissed.

"You mean projecting?" I laughed.

"Fuck you," Devin chuckled. "I hope your dick can't make it pass her cheeks."

Honestly that was a good one, but all it did was make me think about Brittany. Goddamn she had an ass on her. It sat high and wide. It wasn't perfectly round but instead that muhfucka looked like a teardrop. Which was fitting because the day I got to touch her I was definitely going to cry. Suddenly my social battery depleted. Now all I wanted to do was go home and aggressively beat off to the memory of that almost kiss.

My dick twitched against my thigh in confirmation. I guess it was time for that beginning of the end conversation.

"Alright, I–"
"Wait, ain't that your girl?" Devin asked.

As if I summoned her from my mind, Brittany stood in the doorway with a few of her friends. Her skin danced with silver body glitter that contrasted the black slip dress she was wearing. Her makeup consisted of bright eyes smudged in metallic blue with a dark brown lip, and her natural hair was out, spiraling around her heart shaped face. She looked like a wet dream come to life.
"You should ask her to dance," Devin said, pulling me back from my indecent thoughts.
You know how people always consult the devil on their shoulder? Well for me, that devil was Devin. He'd known about my crush on Brittany for years now and each time I swore her off, he'd laugh and say,
"You're gonna put that lady through a mattress one of these days. I'm not tripping off you."
I hate to admit it, but based on the way she dressed, tonight could've very well been that night.

"That's not appropriate," I said, forcing my eyes away from her.
I was trying to school my emotions but then I heard her magical laugh and all the hair on my body stood up, begging me to seek out the source of such a pleasurable sound.
"Nigga, you're pulling a Hallmark on this lady by leaving her gifts everywhere and you probably beat off to her company profile picture once a week. We're way past appropriate. Stop thinking so much and go live a little," he chided.

Fuck, he had several points.
Plus other men were starting to stare and I ain't like that.

"Aight, I'm going," I said, finishing the rest of my drink.
I glided across the room like a moth enamored by the glow of a flame. My eyes were fixed on her and nothing else. She must have sensed it though because as soon as I reached my halfway point we locked gazes. She didn't look away even as her friends were chatting, and we watched each other until I reached her table.
"Hi, Brit," I said with desire pooling in my voice.
My heart was racing from simply looking at her. I don't think God could've crafted a more perfect woman. Sweet, brown, and thick. She was the human equivalent of mo-lasses.
And I wanted a taste.

"Hi, Dimi," she purred while sipping her lemon drop.
Her friends froze, exchanging a look and silently approving of my presence. I'd seen other men get slandered in group chats so I didn't take that for granted. Plus either luck or the DJ must've been on my side because then the perfect song started playing.
"Would you like to dance?" I asked as Be Mine poured over the speakers.
Oh's and Girrrllll's bounced from her friends as we held eye contact, which Brittany only broke to wave them off.
"Shush!" she chided before rising from the table and tak-ing my hand.
"Yeah, I'd like to dance."

A few nearby men wore their wounded pride on their faces as I led Brittany to the dance floor. Be Mine was halfway done, but we still had enough time to fall into a steady rhythm with each other. The glitter on her skin twinkled with each sway of her hips and I soon realized I could watch her dance all night long without needing anything else.

"You look nice tonight," I said softly.

"So do you," she replied, throwing her arms over my shoulders as the tempo of the next song picked up. "Although I didn't take you for a gold chain, open-shirt type."

She brushed her fingertips across my exposed collarbone to touch a link on my chain, but her hand stayed there well after her examination was complete. I hissed in a breath, silently letting her know she wasn't playing fair. To which she replied with a teasing smile.

That was ok though because two could play at that game. I pulled her closer, letting my desire rest against her satin-wrapped thighs, and that's when I noticed she wasn't wearing a bra. Her nipples pebbled against the thin sheath of her dress, tightening and inviting me to take notice.

And take notice I did.

If we weren't in the club I would've taken them into my mouth.

The heels she had on made her the perfect height to do just that. Devin could say what he wanted about me being short, but this shit was an advantage nine times out of ten.

"Damn, not he went and found a skyscraper," someone hollered while we danced.

I sure did. What's not to like about trees? I wasn't bothered, but Brittany looked embarrassed.

"Sorry, heels probably weren't the best thing for us to be dealing with," she mumbled.

"Don't apologize," I said firmly, stroking her back with my free hand. "Besides, I'm not afraid of heights, Brit."

Her cheeks deepened with a slightly noticeable blush that reflected in her eyes.

"What's wrong?" I asked as she focused on our feet, choosing not to meet my eyes for the first time that evening.

I didn't realize that my hands had been resting on her hips until she stroked my left wrist with the pad of her thumb. I slowly loosened my grip but instead of finding purchase in a safer area, my hands traveled to the small of her back and the bottom of her nape. Happy to caress her there and reinforce my growing desire. Her eyes lowered again while she answered me,

"What happened to the shy HR lead who I sometimes share coffee with?"

I laughed, realizing this was the first time she was seeing that I was a whole nother person outside of those white walls.

"He's hanging in the closet with the bowties until Monday morning. Tonight you just get Dimi who wears gold chains and prefers his bourbon straight. Is that alright with you?" I asked.

"It's more than alright," she nodded as I spun her in a lazy circle.

We danced for about thirty minutes before we both needed a drink. Then we retreated to the bar in a fit of laughter and easy conversation. I noticed both of our accompanying parties watching us, Devin sending me an approving smirk and Brittany's friend Kelia giggling every time her and Brit made eye contact. It was weird being on the other side of a very obvious matchmaking attempt, but it was sweet.

"So wait, you introduced Maria and Pepper to each other?" Brittany asked in shock.

Maria and Pepper, two sweet as can be marketing agents, had just celebrated their one year wedding anniversary. I introduced them three years ago.

"Mhm," I nodded. "I knew they'd be perfect together and I was right."

"So you're just an office cupid?" she laughed.

"Basically."

"Mm."

Brittany took a sip of her second lemon drop before leaning across the counter, snagging a cherry from out of a cocktail bowl, and dipping it into my drink with her delicate pointer finger.

"Who else do you think would be perfect together?" she asked, sultry and low.

She held my gaze while wrapping her tongue around the juicy, bright red fruit. I watched shamelessly as she took the entire thing into her mouth and tied the stem into a knot. A knot very similar to the one I'd twist her in if she didn't stop fucking with me.

"Brittany," I warned while trying to dispel the need in my voice.

"Mr. Karimi," she replied, taking a sip of my drink and swirling a piece of ice around with her perfect pink tongue.

Dimitrius was fine. Dimi was preferred when it came to Brittany. But Mr. Karimi? That was too close to Sir, which was really just another way to say Daddy. Brittany was playing with me, testing my boundaries, seeing how far she could take it. Unfortunately she'd hit a wall though. Because I was a covetous man by nature, hearing her eventual last name spill over her lips so freely did something to me.

There was nothing subtle or poetic about what happened next. I rose from my stool, settled my restless body against hers, and captured Brittany's mouth in mine. What came after was a kiss so mind blowing that I once again considered getting down on one knee right there, against the cola-sticky bar tile. Brittany's lips were impossibly soft, pliant, and warm. Her breath carried the tang of fresh fruit and the slight chill of the chewed ice as well as her own addicting taste, and when her tongue swept past her lips to greet mine I slipped even further into the abyss. Before long i was sucking her tongue like it was a fruit bomb pop fresh off the truck.

I realized I was dipping her backwards to earn better access when her hands braced my forearms for support. Her nails sunk into my skin while my greedy fingers were busy lacing through the springy curls located at the back of her neck. It was bad enough I'd lost my carefully curated sense of control, but then she moaned into my mouth. The pleased gasp rang through all my thoughts and that's when I realized I was teetering on the edge of a dangerously steep cliff.

"Mhm, nuhuh," I grunted, pulling away.

My mind was running wild with possibilities. I was so far gone from reality that I had to press my forehead against hers to ground myself. Only for the intoxicating scent of her warm skin to nullify any potential positive effects.

"Did I do something wrong?" she asked softly while looking at me with those soft puma eyes.

My dick developed its own heartbeat when she batted her eyelashes.

"No," I answered roughly while caressing her arm. "This has all been very right."

"Then what's the problem, Dimi?" she whispered while resting her thumb against my bottom lip.

Honestly, I was seconds away from fucking her into the bar. That was the problem.

Understanding the whys of human nature didn't make me any less prone to human needs and impulses. It just changed how I handled them. And Brittany Barnes would see every inch of my need if I wasn't careful.

"Go back over there with your friends before your night ends early," I chuckled before nipping her finger.

Defiance made visible by the glowing neon signage surged in her eyes, making it harder and harder for me to stay on track. I could tell by the way her eyes challenged mine that she'd be all bark and no bite, difficult, and bossy, and I'd love every second of breaching those walls.

Figuratively and literally.

"What if I want it to end?" Brittany asked. "Did you ever think about that, Mister?"

"Brittany, stop playing with me before you end up comatose well into Tuesday morning," I said firmly.

Her throat flexed with a swallow as she met my darkening gaze. Seeing that I wasn't laughing, she produced a well-mannered nod.

"Goodnight Dimi," she said, lips trembling with the urge to incite another kiss between us.

"You won't be able to wear that dress in public anymore if you kiss me again. Good night, Brittany," I said longingly.

She settled for kissing my cheek before I walked her back to the safety of her friends, staining my jaw with brown lipstick, soaked cherries, and the sensation of her. I paid my tab and headed for the door not even a minute later, and Devin whisked out behind me.

"Jesus Christ, Meech. When's the baby shower?" he teased.

My blood boiled from the heat of the memories, igniting my entire body on fire and making me regret my expert level of self control.

"Ask me next Sunday," I gritted, more determined than ever.

Brittany

My right index finger traced the seam of my lips where his tongue probed while my left hand massaged the same patch of now-braided curls that he'd been so busy with. My face flooded with warmth recalling how right it felt melting into his arms and tasting his skin. We melded together perfectly like melody and harmony. His hot hard strength and my yielding softness. My teasing and his chasing. His big dick and my big booty. The possibilities were endless.

Because Dimitrius Karimi was nasty.

And maybe even a soft dom.

"Helloooo, Earth to Brittany?" Sam said, snapping her fingers in front of my eyeline.

"What?" I replied, jumping back into reality.

"Kelia asked which dress you're wearing? What is going on with you?"

"She's thinking about Saturday," Kelia giggled while wiggling her brows.

"Wait, what happened Saturday?" Sam exclaimed.

Saturday.

I woke up, had a big hot breakfast with my parents and sister, decorated our family tree, went to pick up my dry cleaning, searched Lowe's for clearance plants, and then I went home.

Put on a little dress.

Put on some sparkly makeup.

Drove to the club with my homegirls.

Saw the man who was my mentally-appointed work husband looking good as fuck with his chest out.

Danced with him.

Almost got folded like a Dollar General lawn chair after that.

"Um," I started.

Sam was waiting expectedly. Standing off to the side with her arms crossed over her chest like a crotchety teacher surviving off too little pay and too much coffee. But right before I could fully reply, the answer walked in.

"Dimi," I gasped.

"Hey, Brit. Do you have a second?" he asked.

I'm not new to corporate code-switching and work per-sonalities by any means, but Dimitrius was so good at it that it was scary. The hard, longing edge he spoke with Saturday was replaced with a completely respectful, professional, cadence. One that would never threaten to fuck me into a weekend coma. His chest was put away, his gaze wasn't dripping with lust, and even his smile was sanitized. It wasn't the same deadly grin I saw taunting me under the neon club lights. Not even close.

"Brittany?" he called again, snapping me out of my trance.

"Oh, shit. That's me," I giggled anxiously. "How- What was the question again?"

Something wicked briefly flashed in his eyes before he obliged me.

"Do you have a minute? Catering is coming tomorrow to discuss station layouts, but I was going to handle it since you have a meeting right in the middle of their service window."

That's right, they wanted to make sure the serving sta-tions weren't going to affect the decorations. I had gotten the email this morning but decided to wait until I could figure out the scheduling conflict to reply. Yet somehow, Dimi had already handled it.

I wondered what else he could handle.

Especially with those big hands.

"Of course, Dimitrius," I nodded.

"Mmph," Kelia scoffed from her position on my tripod.

"I gotta go," I said, pulling my phone from the bracket and hovering my thumb over the big red button that was probably going to save my life.

"Mhm, I heard him. Call me after you *cum* to-"
I hung up on her and flipped my phone over as if that was going to change what just happened. It didn't, but I didn't need the evidence to be right in my face.

Dimi leaned against the wall housing my desk with a dangerous amount of confidence. Confidence that could only come from testimonials. He held my gaze, daring me to deny what we'd both just heard, but I couldn't. I definitely wanted to nut on that perfect, handsome face.
"Sam, could you give us a minute?" I said, holding eye contact with Dimitrius.
"I'll give you sixty," Sam said warily. "I put condoms in the top drawer."
"Sam!" I hissed as she slipped out the door.
"Thanks, Boss!" she laughed with a wave.

Damn her for reading my bucket list! Desk sex was action item number 10. But that wasn't Dimi's business.
The door shut behind her with a click and my shoulders tightened with my sorrowful grimace.
"Sorry about that. You were saying?"
I held my breath, expecting to see a glimpse of the man I danced with on Saturday. I even poked my chest out, hoping he'd say what he really wanted to say.
"No worries, I sent an email with some suggestions I had. Do you want to go over it?" he asked instead.
I chewed my bottom lip while opening the email. As usual when dealing with Dimitrius, it was perfect. I had very little feedback but I was still going to take up his time. Even if he was busy avoiding the elephant in the room by playing a very big game of pretend.

"Yeah, take a seat," I replied, turning my monitor outward. "I just have a few things."

We chatted for one glorious hour. Dimi made a 3D model of the ballroom and we used that to configure our table arrangement. We had lots of good dialogue about why Samson and Margie should be at least ten feet apart all night. But when we got towards the end, I stopped talking and just listened instead. Mostly because even with his work guards on, Dimi still had the smoothest, most animated voice I'd ever had the pleasure of hearing. His lips parted with such fluidity, drawing me in while aiding his perfect annunciation. His strong jaw flexed beautifully with every long syllable and exaggerated laugh. That's when I realized I was lost in his speech, but I wasn't listening to a damn thing.

"What's on your mind, Brit?" Dimi asked with a sly chuckle.
I tried to dismiss his question with a laugh but my tongue was glued to the roof of my mouth. That's when I finally realized I was staring and mouth breathing.
Busted.
Trying to play it off, I retreated back into my own bubble and shrugged.
"Why do you think something is on my mind?" I queried, trying to sound nonchalant.
Failing at sounding nonchalant.
Dimi watched me silently for a few beats before spreading his elbows across the espresso oak desktop. He stopped inches from my face, making sure our gazes were aligned.
"Because your mouth is quiet but your eyes aren't," he

chuckled. "So tell me, what are you thinking about Ms. Barnes?"

Right then I was thinking about how to appear normal even though my heart was racing like a formula 1 car. But that was until I saw the gleam of his chain peeking out the collar of his button-up. That little sliver of personality cutting through his careful corporate charade reminded me instantly. I was now thinking about how artfully he slid his tongue over my canines.

"Saturday," I answered.

"Oh yeah?" Dimi smiled. "What happened Saturday?"

"You kissed me Saturday," I said softly.

His lips parted like he was going to give me a recap and I was all too eager to lean in. But instead of pressing his mouth against mine, he slowly reached forward to let his thumb rest against my bottom lip.

"And tell me, Ms. Barnes, how did that make you feel?" he asked with a gravelly voice.

How did the best kiss of my life make me feel?

Oh this man.

My words dried up but my poor pussy flooded. I couldn't speak. I couldn't think. All I could do was stare and hope he'd grant me some mercy.

"Brittany."

"Hm?" I hummed absentmindedly.

"I asked you a question, gorgeous. How did that make you feel?"

Listen, we were already toeing a thin line with the extended lunches, inside jokes, and coffee breaks, but the weekend prior had thinned it even further. Actually if I'm being honest, it crossed the original line and formed an X.

Which could either stand for buried treasure or rightful termination, but either way I had decided I was fine with it.

"It made me feel good," I purred in response.
Who was I kidding? That shit made my womanhood quiver.
Shout out to my bitch Helga.
I could've told him that, but that's the problem with society these days: We don't keep enough secrets. I was trying to change that. Starting now.
"Just good?" Dimi queried while his brown eyes filled with deep, suffocating desire.
His chest rose and fell rapidly, like he was a man on a mission. Or a predator on the hunt for prey.
"Yeah, good," I confirmed with a simple nod.

Dimitrius' eyes flickered with a challenge, one that promised to change my mind about my affections. And oh, how I wanted him to. I wanted him to prove me right. So terribly right.
We slowly grew closer, like plants vining out in search of sunlight. Then with the gentlest touch to the back of my neck, he brought my mouth to his. The hands on the clock ceased to advance while we shared more than air. I relished the complex taste of his skin. Tea with lemon, peppermints, and what I can only describe as materialized lust. Dimitrius tasted like heaven.

Then I placed my hand against his chest while trying to get even closer and he moaned, husky and heavy.
He sounded like heaven too.
"Brittany," he pleaded. "We need to stop before I take it

too far."

"What's too far?" I responded breathlessly before seeking his lips again.

He obliged me only to stop again when I slid my hand down his open collar and caressed his moisturized skin.

"Fucking you into this desk and keeping you quiet by gagging you with a candy cane would be too far. And that's exactly where we're headed," he warned with delirious laughter.

"Dimi, you wouldn't," I gasped.

"Oh, I absolutely would," he said while holding my jaw to stare into my eyes.

His big thumb swept over the apex of my chin with tender strokes, making me dizzy with affection. I always knew Dimi was a secret softie but experiencing it up close and very personal had me giddy. Even though he threatened to rearrange my guts over my heirloom desk.

I could tell he was serious from The Great Pyramid Of Giza model tenting his pants. He had more rise than The Jefferson's deluxe apartment in the sky.

"Are you going to share with the class, Mister Karimi?" I purred, motioning to his print.

"Not this time," Dimitrius replied while kissing my nose. "I'll see you Saturday, Brittany."

"Dimi," I whined. "But that's so far away."

He rose from the chair across from me, stretched onto his toes, then repositioned the bulge in his pants so it wouldn't poke my eye out before sanitizing his hands.

"Somehow I think you'll make it, Brit," he chuckled. "You've always been so patient with everyone around you, so I know you can be patient for me. Can't you, pretty girl?"

I swear I heard the dial-up noise for a solid ten seconds before my brain successfully rebooted itself. I knew Dimitrius was dangerous, but that sentence was just outright toxic. I felt like Saturday had the potential to change the trajectory of my life if I wasn't careful. Something told me that Dimi was the type of man women keyed cars over. That was a bummer because I preferred my nails long, and long nails didn't work with a potential future in vandalism.

Oh well though.

I managed a nod and I was rewarded with a rich, handsome smile.

God I loved Dimi's smile. It was like watching the sun rise.

I was so completely smitten that I didn't even notice Sam's shadow creeping against the frosted glass until Dimitrius opened the door and she came tumbling over the threshold.

"Tuh," Dimi chuckled. "Don't worry, you didn't miss anything."

"I wasn't listening," Sam protested while straightening her shirt. "I just wanted confirmation on how you were wearing your hair Saturday. So I can book your appointment with Ms. Diane."

I shot her a challenging brow raise. Somehow I remained unconvinced even though that was Sam's job on paper.

"Promise," she said, raising her right hand with a smile.

"Mhm, ok," I tutted. "But hold off on scheduling the appointment please. I still don't know what I want to do with my hair."

I had figured out the dress, the shoes, the jewelry, the limited edition holographic Zaza Bag, but I was still very much undecided on my hair. Honestly I needed a break from wigs, but I didn't want to sit in anybody's chair for braids, and me and weaves had never gotten along. That didn't leave many options left.

"You should wear it-" Sam started.
"Natural," Dimi finished. "Like Saturday."
I stared at him and his overly pleased smile until my watering eyes forced me to blink. Normally I'd curse someone out for hinting at my personal business, but instead of being irritated I felt kind of excited. Who was this man and what was he doing to me?
"Ok seriously, what happened on Saturday?" Sam shrieked.
"Ask Brittany," Dimitrius said with a shrug. "I'm sure she'd love to tell you all about it."
And then he left.
"So Saturday?" Sam sang with a smirk, sitting the mail on my desk.

I rolled my eyes and picked up the small packages she brought, running my nails across the taut line of tape.
"It was nothing," I scoffed. "Dimi just saw me out with the girls and bought me a drink."
"That didn't seem like nothing," Sam countered. "You could scoop the tension between you guys with a spoon. So what happened? Did you guys..." she said, making the motion with her hands.
"Sam!" I chided.
I jerked and the box in my hands fell against the desk, causing the contents to spill out. I thought I was opening

place cards for Saturday, but it was actually another gift. A birthstone necklace in the shape of a B.

4
Two In The Bush

Dimitrius

You'd never know Christmas was supposed to be in four days based on the temperature. It was hot and humid. The sun was bright and persistent. The air was thick and it clung to your skin like cheap lotion. I'm looking at you, Queen Helene. But despite that, Christmas was very much in the air at Solei's headquarters. Every palm tree and thorny shrub had its trunk wrapped in bright twinkling lights while garland hung from the branches. The main entrances were decorated with grand wreaths hanging overhead accompanied by big strawberry red velvet bows tied on the doors, and a Christmas playlist to end all Christmas playlists could be heard from the nearby sidewalk.

Brittany had gone all out.

"It looks great in here, Brit," I said as I entered the ball-room.

Brittany stood in the center of the room, directing the caterer's dessert set up. She was dressed casually and it was my first time seeing her in just sweats and a tee. Her hair was tied up in a patterned silk scarf, and she had on a pair of limited edition Winter Solstice dunks in place of her heels. What I'm trying to say is she looked absolutely gorgeous. Luckily I didn't have to hide that I felt that way anymore.

"Thank you, Dimi," she cooed excitedly. "The chairs really tied it all together."

Even if we were to completely disregard the entrance, the ballroom had metamorphosed into a grand winter wonderland. Ornaments of varying heights and shapes hung from the ceiling with invisible thread, making them appear as if they were floating. Tables were lined with sumptuous velvet tablecloths and arranged with crystal silverware, gold and red chargers in an alternating pat-tern, with large nutcrackers at the center surrounded by hardy winter bouquets trimmed with frosty sugarplums. Then don't even get me started about the lights. They were everywhere, but the effect was subtle. They glowed soft warm light with a gentle flickering pulse. Reminding me of candlelight.

"Brit, I know they were important to you, but fuck those chairs. Nobody is walking in here and looking at those chairs," I mumbled with my eyes to the ceiling.

She scoffed but it was true. The chairs would be the least interesting looking thing in the room tonight. Because instead they'd be looking at the twenty-foot Christmas tree in the back of the room, or the countless bows, or the ornate foiled place cards. At that moment I knew I'd spare no expense for our inevitable wedding. Brittany would have whatever her heart desired. I didn't care if she wanted a yacht.

"We worked so hard for those chairs, Dimi," she pouted.

Her bottom lip poked out and I wanted so terribly to kiss it back into place, but I was sure that'd end our night young if I had.

"I'm sorry, I just don't want you to discount all your other hard work, sweetheart," I said while brushing my hand against hers.

Yeah I slid that sweetheart in there. Mostly because I wanted to test Brittany's reaction to it, and also to let her know that absolutely nothing had changed from Monday. Yes I had on a bowtie, but that wouldn't be the only thing wrapped around my neck before the night's end if I could help it.

"I-I," she stammered. "I need to go change."

"Go ahead," I said, gently kissing her hand which was still entangled with mine. "I'll handle the rest of the setup."

Her face flushed, her cheeks subtly darkening, and then she looked away. She sunk her upper canine into her soft lower lip to suppress what I now knew was a smile. It didn't work, but instead of fighting it further, she let it reach her eyes.

"Well then I leave everything in your very capable hands, Dimi," she purred.

It was the weekend and no one else was around besides the party vendors. That left Brittany feeling emboldened, so she leaned in close, brushing her lips against my neck. "I'll see you later."
One thing for sure, two things for certain, she'd definitely be seeing me later. Much later. She wanted to play games and I had an arcade.
Game. Set. Match.

Brittany

It felt very serendipitous that Dimi's bowtie matched my dress, down to the fabric and shade. Serendipitous or something else...
"How long have you known about Dimitrius' crush on me?" I asked Sam.
She finished zipping up my dress with a hearty sigh.
"I had my suspicions ever since he started bypassing the second floor breakroom to have coffee in ours. Especially when I figured out there's a perfect view of your office from there," Sam admitted.
I nearly bit through my bottom lip. Dimi had been using the fourth floor break room for at least a year. I thought it was just because he preferred our creamer selection. Not because he wanted to taste *my* creamer.
"Why didn't you say anything?" I chided.

I wasn't mad at Sam, but I was feeling like the last one to find out and I ain't like that at all. She was basically telling me I could've sat on Dimi's face months ago had I not been so oblivious and hung up on professionalism.
"Well at first I thought he was trying to fire you. But I was woefully incorrect," she sighed. "He's just infatuated."

Suddenly, I remembered what I was looking for. A type-A lover boy. A man who would probably organize caterers by three different categories starting with cuisine type. A man who would probably preemptively check my meeting schedule to see if there were any conflicts with the service windows. A man who knew me well enough to know I didn't drink caffeine after 10am…

"Sam!" I shouted just as my phone rang.

"Oh, it's Kelia!" Sam replied, handing me my phone from the desk.

I didn't even have a chance to ask any follow up questions after that because Sam conveniently slid out of the room as soon as I answered Kelia's call.

She was slicker than a peeled onion.

"Hey, friend! Ooh you look so pretty!" she exclaimed as I did my obligatory twirl.

"Thanks," I gritted, fluffing my roots out a little more.

"What's wrong? Why you sound pissed off?"

I stomped my foot against the carpet, huffing and puffing with every aggravated movement. I knew I was being childish because I could hear my grandma's lecture on acting my age in my ear the whole time, but I couldn't help it.

"I think I just got played by my assistant and the head of HR," I explained.

"Wait, the guy you were dancing with last Saturday and Sam are fucking? I know she ain't do no foul shi-"

"No, they're not fucking!" I interjected as the imagery upset my spirit. "I-I think she knew he was my secret santa this whole time and ain't say anything."

"Well duh," Kelia laughed. "Ain't nobody getting past Sam.

But it wouldn't be a secret if you knew who it was, now would it?"

"Kelia! Whose side are you on?"

"Yours of course, Brit," she said sweetly. "Except this time. You suck the fun out of surprises. You got control issues bad, baby girl."

I stood there with my mouth gaping like an out-of-water catfish. Just looking and fuming. This was the third time I'd heard that in a month. At this point it felt like the default response.

"I do not suck the fun out of surprises!" I scoffed.

"Mhm, except you definitely do. You accidentally found out about your sweet sixteen and basically took over planning with "subtle" suggestions. I think Sam was right not to tell you who your secret santa daddy is. It's clear that man is trying to court you and you would've made him stop, returned the gifts, or forced him into something practical. Enjoy the holiday magic for once!"

I closed my mouth and silenced my rebuttal when I realized she was right. Had I found out it was Dimi, I probably would've returned everything and made him take me out for a simple dinner instead. He obviously knew me well enough to know that. So maybe Kelia, Sam, and Daddy were right. Maybe I did suck the fun out of surprises.

"I don't try to you know," I whispered.

"Yeah, I know. You just don't like disappointment. Join the club," Kelia shrugged. "But I doubt Santa Daddy is going to disappoint you. So get off the phone and go get your man, girl. Them titties sitting up like two cantaloupes. Your time is now."

I knew Kelia was right because my modest c-cups were

damn near tickling my collar bones. God bless boob tape I guess.

"You may be right about this one little thing, but don't think I'm letting Sam off the hook!" I chided with a pointed finger.

Kelia fixed her blanket around her sides with a smile.

"Leave Sam alone. She did what any good assistant would do. She got you some dick delivered for Christmas. Give her an extended weekend and a big hug. I gotta go, my show is on. Bye, love youuu," Kelia sang, ending our call.

I rolled my eyes as her picture faded from my screen and then used my camera to touch up my lipstick.

I caught a glimpse of my silhouette when I turned to put my lipstick back in my bag,

Damn.

Kelia was right, I did look good.

Real good.

I was still mad about being played by Sam and possibly Dimi, but I checked the left hand side of the upper desk drawer before I went downstairs to give them a piece of my mind. Despite everything I had to admit Sam was always prepared. She was a damn good assistant.

5
It Never Snows In LA

I was never aware of how resounding it was when my heels clicked against hard floors until now. Every heavy tap mirrored the beating of my anxious heart. Especially when I got on the elevators. The reflective panels forced me to focus on what was about to happen. After years of quiet looks, inconspicuous smiles, and shared coffee breaks I was about to do it.

I was about to fuck the head of Human Resources.

The whole ride down I'd been thinking about what I would say to Dimi. Maybe I'd call him out. Maybe I'd play dumb a little longer. Or maybe a secret third thing. Which would probably be me melting into his arms like I did the Saturday previous after failing to tough talk him. I don't know what it was about his non-professional nigga voice, but it could strongarm me smooth up out of my undergarments.

The elevator dinged and I had finally settled on something I thought would be a good mix of all three of those options, but as soon as I stepped foot into the ballroom I was swarmed. It had only been an hour since I left to get ready and we already had a full house. As the COO, lots of people were trying to start or foster a networking relationship. It was a responsibility that came with the job so I couldn't be mad at it, but I'll be damned if it wasn't inconvenient as hell. Dimi was chatting with a vendor when I got down there and by time I made it through the fourth handshake and greeting he had disappeared.

Dinner didn't make it any easier. The food was excellent because Dimi knew what the fuck he was talking about. Unfortunately, however, he and I were sitting at different tables, respective to our departments, and every time a seat freed up next to one of us, some unknowing jackass filled it. I couldn't have my white Christmases any more so this glittery twinkly night should've been everything I wanted. Instead I was just frustrated and praying for it to end. Right until the Customer Operations Lead left and someone new sat besides me with a steaming bowl of macaroni. Macaroni piled high with brisket, green onions, and barbecue sauce.
Someone with a broad smile and dark eyes.

"Hi, you looked like you could use some company," Dimi said, offering me the mac.
"Oh, did I look lonely?" I chuckled.

"Mhm, a real wallflower. Robinson didn't even ask to see your dance card."
"What is this? 1863?"
"No, but if it was then I'd have to tell you, dear Brittany, that Robinson would make a terrible match for you," Dimi said, adopting a pretty convincing English accent.
"On what basis, Lord Karimi?" I giggled, matching his speech.
"Well for one, my lady. He's much too tall for you. He'd most certainly hog a bed, never mind the covers. Plus you'd always have to hear about his "life altering" back pain."
I snorted into my open palm which startled the accountant lead to my right. But I didn't care, it was a good laugh.

"Plus he has a notable aversion to carbohydrates, madam. You enjoy your rice with a side of mashed potatoes. That'd be a match most horrible indeed," he smiled.
I giggled before taking a bite of Dimi's Mac. He didn't cook it, but it still carried that same magical hand taste. Creamy, rich, and balanced. Happiness in a cup.
I sat aside that happiness temporarily to pursue another kind. A more lasting happiness.

"Who do you think would be my perfect match then?" I asked.
"Well for one, he ought to know how much you adore peppermint mocha in the winter, and respect your equal, yet insidious love for mint chip ice cream in the summer."
"Ooh, good point," I nodded.
"Mhm," Dimi said, tucking a stray curl behind my ear. "He

should also be versed in natural hair care. Because wash day will inevitably become a group effort. And he should know that you like matching your claw clips to your shoes and handbags."

Damn he was good.

I went with a sheer seamless thong but I was starting to regret even that. Dimitrius deserved it hot and ready. No gimmicks, no tricks.

"Anything else?" I whispered.

"Yes," Dimi nodded with his lips pressed tight into a grave line. "I also think your perfect match is someone who's obsessed with how your eyes twinkle in the sunlight. Someone who gets high off your laugh. Someone who knows how much you hate Mondays, and how much you love late mornings. Someone who would love nothing more than to hold you until the sun declares midday."

Our future was immediately clear to me. Lazy, intimate mornings, laughter filled evenings, and all the beautiful possibilities in between. It might've been the Christmas magic but it felt like a dream. A vivid premonition of what was to come.

"Dimitrius," I cooed in disbelief.

"I really really like you, Brittany," he replied, almost reading my mind. "Like real bad."

"I really really like you too," I giggled. "Also real bad."

The cool mysterious exterior of Dimitrius Karimi crumbled with a nervous smile. One that tucked the left corner of his lip under his canine. He really was the total package. Fine, humble, and sweet as pie. I meant it when I said

God wasn't making them like this anymore. Yet somehow I'd gotten blessed with a limited edition to call my own.

"Will you do me the honor of this dance, Ms. Barnes?" Dimitrius asked as the intro to Sweet Love played over the speakers.
I didn't miss the fact that my Christmas extravaganza playlist got exchanged for one of my favorite songs.
"I thought you'd never ask, Mr. Karimi, Sir," I smiled.
He led me to the center of the dance floor by my hand, gently stroking my knuckles the entire time. He was as graceful as he was gentle and I half-expected anoth-er sanitized version of last Saturday. But then just as the beat dropped and Anita's sensual vocals flooded the speakers, my body was pulled tight against his. There was nothing respectful about the way he held me or the rhythm in his hips.

"Dimi," I whispered as he spun me. "Is this a preview of what is hopefully happening tonight?"
Because if it was I needed to start looking at bridal gowns.
"Brittany, don't make me blush," Dimi chuckled while dip-ping me. "Them people are already staring at us."
Of course those people were staring. Hell, if this had been a school dance I'm sure we would've evoked the wrath of a chaperone with the very first swivel. This was the kind of gyration teenage pregnancies were made of.
"So what? I'm their boss. Let them stare," I replied. "We look good together."
"Yeah?"
"Yeah," I nodded.
"Well then let's make this memorable," he chuckled.

The holiday playlist was back, and this time Baby-face's White Christmas played over the sound system. I blinked and suddenly the room was filled with soft, fluffy snowflakes. The crowd gasped and cheered as they cascaded down like a materialized dream and gathered on the ends of my curls and eyelashes. Music was playing but I was frozen in time, mesmerized by the sheer impossibility of it all.

I was getting a white Christmas after fifteen years. A first since my daddy packed us up and moved us to LA. A true surprise.

"Did yo- did you do this?" I gasped through welling tears.

I had mentioned missing the snow back home once in the last seven years, and somehow he remembered. I couldn't believe it.

"Do you like it? Did I do too much?" he asked nervously.

I saw the anticipation rise in Dimi's eyes. He held his breath while waiting for mine. The man I knew as a pillar of confidence for the past seven years transformed before my very eyes into someone so vulnerable and beautiful. That's when I finally realized Dimitrius Karimi was probably in love with me.

The room around us vanished as I pressed my hand against his heart and leaned in for a kiss. His lips yielded to mine, allowing me to take as much as I wanted without issue. His hands, which were previously placed at the top of my back, slid to the curve of my spine and pressed me closer, encouraging me to soften against him. I let my right hand explore the plains of his nearest shoulder blade, but when I tickled the exposed skin of his neck with my fingertips, he pulled away.

"Brittany, they're gonna fire us if you touch me like that," he warned, voice low and raw.

Part of me wanted to laugh, but the other part of me, the one who remembered last Saturday, knew he was deadly serious. Unfortunately, not even the threat of termination could deter me. Not even from the head of Human Resources himself. I wanted to unravel his tie and sink my nails into the flesh underneath it. Luckily I had plenty of practice unwrapping tight packages thanks to him.

"Help me with something in my office?" I whispered breathlessly.

Dimi nodded wordlessly and followed me to the elevators with low eyes. Luckily the bar was open so no one paid us much attention besides that initial dance. They were too busy enjoying a night on the company, which I fully supported. Especially since it meant I could have my cake and eat it too.

I wasn't one for impatience, but as soon as we made it to the hall, I mashed the elevator button like I was going for gold in Family Feud. I was so dizzy from our kiss that I couldn't truthfully tell if my current position was a dream or some kind of magic-induced reality and I was also unwilling to wait and find out. The sooner I could get my hands on that man, the better. Until the elevator dinged.

"Brittany Barnes, just the woman I was hoping to see!"

I had heard the rumors but I didn't think it'd happen to me personally. After all, we were only four days out from Christmas. However that didn't matter because Marvin Rosenbloom had popped by anyway.

"Mister Rosenbloom, Sir! It's great to see you!" I exclaimed, straightening my posture and extending my hand. Unfortunately I was still dizzy from all the hormones flooding my body and that quick motion affected my balance and threatened to send me toppling forward. Luckily though, Dimi caught me. Unluckily, he caught me by my waist.

"Marvin, dear. I think we're interrupting," the woman by his side interjected.

She was a tiny lady with cognac colored skin, huge hair, and an equally huge ring. She was stunning and her lips were decorated with the proof of a thousand smiles and lipstick that matched the shade staining my boss's neck. The rumors didn't do Winifred Rosenbloom justice. And she was as perceptive as she was beautiful.

"Oh," Marvin said in surprise.

Whether it was good or bad surprise, I couldn't tell, but I was doing damage control regardless.

"Mister Rosenbloom, I can explain," I offered.

He exchanged a look with Dimi and laughed.

"No need, Brittany. I just wanted to congratulate you on the beautiful party. But I like this," he laughed, pointing between us. "This is good."

"Oh," I sighcd with a hearty dose of confusion.

The employee handbook was clear as day, no relationships between management and subordinates were allowed. I just knew he was about to have security fetch us a couple of boxes. But that wasn't happening.

"Martin's a bleeding heart, dear," Winifred explained, patting her husband's chest. "A real sucker for romance."

"I am," he conceded with a sigh. "I also like weddings if you two are by any chance planning to have one."

Winifred rolled her eyes and pulled Marvin off the elevator with a chuckle,

"Marvin, that's a terrifying proposition. Leave them be and let's go dance."

They left us with a wave before Dimi turned to me with a proud smile.

"He really does like weddings, by the way. He went to Pepper and Maria's. He got them a Ninja Slushie."

"Are you proposing to me on day one, Dimi?" I chuckled.

"No, not right now. As you can see, I prefer to solicit your grace with grand gestures, and I don't have enough time to break ground yet."

Break ground? What did that mean?

"Don't think about it too much," he said softly, lacing his hand in mine. "I just be saying shit."

Instinct and previous experience warned me that probably wasn't true, but I let him have it for now because I was choosing to enjoy the moment.

Somehow the moment turned into a soft porn intro somewhere in the short amount of time it took us to reach the fourth floor. The first few kisses we shared were soft, gentle, full of promise and respect. But once we got the ok from the big boss, that shit went out the window. Dimi was kissing me like he might not be alive the next day. With one of his hands gripping my ass and the other massaging my curls, he led my body through every last one of the seven deadliest sins.

Pride told me that I deserved every second of this and that made way for greed which made my subconscious believe I never had to stop. That made it easy for lust to charge through every fiber of my being and I rolled my hips against his, desperate to feel even more. For a second I was envious of his clothes because I realized they got to touch him all the time. But then Dimi slid his tongue back into my mouth and I became addicted to the taste of him, overindulging in everything he had to offer. That only pissed me off in the end though because I realized I could've had him months earlier if only he'd been more forward. Until I wondered how much I really needed a job because without one I could spend my days wrapped around him.

Somehow we made it to the privacy of my office with all of our clothes intact, but I knew that wouldn't remain the case and Dimi confirmed it as soon as he shut the door behind me. He pinned me against the closest wall and we resumed where we left off.

"May I?" Dimitrius whispered against my swollen lips as his fingers trailed my thigh.

I didn't even notice that my left leg had been hiked around his waist until he separated us. He was practicing re-straint but I could tell by the way he clenched his jaw that he was struggling. Still he remained a gentleman. So to reward him for being a good boy I nodded my agreement and those large deft digits of his immediately swept across the seat of my panties before pulling them to the side. He then carefully traced my slit with the tip of his pointer before adding his middle finger to the mix and sinking them both inside of me.

"Fuck, Brittany," he hissed. "You're so wet, Kbida."

I whimpered as he rolled his hand upward and curled his fingers inside me. Somehow his hand fit perfectly against my sex and he was able to use the heel of his palm to tease my swollen clit while he stroked in and out of me. Then he slipped his thumb into my mouth. The pleasure built up in layers. The first layer from his warm hand caressing my thumping bud, the second from the way his fingers stretched and teased me, and the third from the slight amount of pressure he put on my tongue to keep my mouth occupied and quiet. I'd never experienced foreplay so overwhelming in all my 32 years so my first instinct was to close my eyes when I felt the wave begin to crest, but Dimi squeezed my throat with a gentle warning.

"Eyes on me, sweetheart," he whispered. "Keep those eyes on me, pretty girl."

Just like that I was hypnotized and transfixed. All I could look at was Dimitrius. I focused on the way his brow met when he licked his lips, the depth of his dimples when he flashed me a pleased smile for my obedience, and the primal way his pupils dilated when my climax finally overtook me and I moaned his name. My knees wobbled and gave out due to the sheer force of my release then I slumped against him in a sweaty heap.

"I'm so proud of you," Dimi cooed, kissing my shoulder blade. "You did such a good job."

I smiled in response, but I secretly knew that man would eventually dissolve my sanity. He seemed capable of creating a nutcase and an example out of me.

Oh well though.

I remained tucked against him for a few seconds while I caught my breath. Dimi rubbed my back the entire time with his knuckles rolling over my spine and shoulder blades at a soothing, predictable pace. Eventually my heart rate returned to normal and my skin cooled so I pulled myself upright, but when my vision refocused I was mortified. Because there was another gift on my desk.

I practically ran to scoop up the newest installation, and to my surprise it was a snow globe. But it wasn't just any snow globe. It was an incredibly detailed encapsulation of my hometown. It even contained a miniature version of my childhood terrier, Frodo. I thought the culprit was Dimi but clearly I was wrong. He had been with me the entire time since I'd left the office, and even before we met up at dinner, I was still able to track him down amongst the crowd in the ballroom.

"What the fuck!?" I shrieked while reading the engravement. "Who is doing this?"
"Brittany, what's wrong?" Dimitrius asked.
I spun around to face him with urgency. If it wasn't Dimitrius, but it was someone who knew how to get past Sam, I would need help. I might even need to see if I could have security pull the tapes from the hall camera.
"Listen, this is gonna sound real crazy, but I think I have a stalker. I keep getting gifts, but they're super duper personalized, like blankets, jewelry, and plants, and at first I thought it was you because we got this thing going on, but then this just popped up when we were both downstairs and-"
"Brittany, breathe," Dimitrius said, while rubbing my shoulders.
His voice soothed me instantly and I did as I was told,

inhaling with my belly and exhaling deeply in an effort to prevent an anxiety attack. Over and over until I was calm.

"Firstly, you are correct. These are my gifts," Dimi admitted after a few beats.
"What how?"
"Sam isn't the only one who's tight with facility," he chuckled. "But I'm sorry, I didn't mean to scare you. I was going for Twelve Days Of Christmas. Not Five Nights At Freddy's."
He looked so defeated and although I know it wasn't his intention to make me feel bad, I did. My uptight ass was killing the romance.
"Sorry. I'm not good with surprises," I admitted with a sigh.
"Hey, that's ok," Dimi said softly before cupping my face. "I know that now for the future."
The future. That sounded nice. Also very sincere. Then there was the small matter of his expert gift giving.

"You really like me, huh?" I snorted.
"Yeah, I really do," he nodded. "And I think you like me too."
I tipped my chin slightly upward in agreement before pressing my mouth to his. I definitely liked Dimitrius Karimi.
I could feel Dimi smiling against my lips with every eager peck. His lashes softly swept against the tops of my cheekbones while the tips of our noses softly rubbed against one another when we pulled away to catch our breath. It was the perfect kiss with the perfect person and I was in heaven. Until I realized I could taste myself on his lips.

"Dimitrius, did you lick your fingers clean?" I gasped.

"I couldn't help myself," he confessed. "You smelled so good and I didn't want to waste it."

He flashed me a hungry smile full of teeth before leading me to my desk.

"Matter of fact, I just remembered something. There's mistletoe hanging off your desk."

There was a mistletoe garland hanging on my desk, but I hadn't realized it until then. I just added it, hoping it would help me feel that Christmas magic that LA lacked. But it was clear that this twisted soul was hoping it would help me feel something else.

"Did you know it's bad luck if you don't get a kiss under the mistletoe?" Dimi asked.

"Even if it's plastic?"

"Even if it's plastic," he confirmed with a nod. "But don't worry, I'm more than happy to help."

I was led to sit in my desk chair, and once I was comfortable, Dimi rolled it all the way back against the wall and took the space in front of it. His smile spread all the way to his ears as his hands gripped the sides of my thighs but then it faltered momentarily as he dug in his pockcts. What the hell was he looking for? Narnia?

"Sorry, I just wanted to make sure you had this before I got started," Dimi explained, producing a wrapped candy cane.

He opened it for me, and with me being the proud show off I am, curled my tongue around the hook and brought it into my mouth, hoping it'd give him a preview of later.

"I hate eating in front of other people without offering them something too," Dimi said innocently. "Anyway, enjoy."

It took him less than three seconds to push my knees to my chest, peel my thong off, and hang my ankles over his shoulders. Immediately after that I had learned the importance of the candy cane. Because without a preoccupation, my big mouth ass would've let the whole company know I found the true meaning of Christmas: Getting head under the mistletoe.

Dimi's tongue was thick and deceptively agile. He brought my clit between his lips with a gentle suck and then flicked the tip of said tongue against it with featherlight pressure. I couldn't moan his name or beg for mercy so I expressed my favor by gripping his shoulders. He took a deep breath, inhaling my scent, and inched forward to meet my demands while my legs spread to accommodate him. Only for me to run out of room and collide with my chair's armrests.

Suddenly I was in a corner with nowhere to run.

"Dimi, wait," I gargled, the pleads sounding foreign.

My begging fell on deaf ears because he continued eating me like I was a banana pudding.

"Dimi, please," I begged while my body writhed around in uncoordinated pleasure. "It's too much. I can't take it."

"Yes you can, Kbida," he replied confidentially. "You can do anything you put your mind to. Such as fuck my face like the good little vixen you are."

See that's where he was wrong because I wouldn't be on anybody's good list after tonight. I was definitely getting coal in my stockings.

So I decided to hush and let that man twirl his tongue in my cat.

"Just like that," I whimpered over my candy cane.

Dimi's grip tightened on my thigh while his free hand crept up to my bust. He drew soft circles around my nipple, teasing me with the occasional pinch, keeping his fingers steady.

Then he moaned into my sex.

I had heard about the fabled men who ate for their own pleasure, but never had I experienced it. I was already close but that husky, raw hum sent my senses into overdrive. I started bucking my hips to chase my release and Dimi took it like a champ. Our pace didn't slow, our rhythm didn't falter, and nor did Dimi's tongue. My orgasm overtook me like a spring twister. Wet, violent, and quick. I was left dizzy and distraught.

I could barely focus my eyes and yet I could still see Dimi's mischievous smile over the top of my heaving chest. He rose, licked his lips, and wiped his sticky face on a tissue before sliding the hook of the candy cane out of my mouth and into his. The gag was a great idea initially, but had I known I would cum so hard that it'd snap in half I would've declined. I probably would've declined the desk head all together if I knew how much trouble Human Resources was.

"Are you a sadist?" I huffed.

My voice trembled under the weight of my fleeting breath, and despite Dimi's insistence that he was in fact, not a sadist, I wasn't convinced. Mostly due to his ever-present smile.

"I'm just nasty, Brit. Plus it's been a while," he explained while helping me up.

Once I was standing, Dimitrius put me back together without me having to lift a finger. My dress was turned back to the front, my jewelry was untwisted, and my hair was fluffed and returned to its curly glory.

"There," Dimi said proudly. "Back to your beautiful Brit self."

"What about my panties?" I asked, noticing them clutched in his fist.

"I think I'll keep these," he replied while pecking my nose. "I earned them, after all."

"Dimitrius!" I chided as he stuffed my undergarments into his pocket.

"Brittany," he teased in return.

His cool smile returned with a vendetta and once again rendered me speechless. The room slowly devolved into a hazy dream starring Dimi. One that focused almost exclusively on the deep Cupid's bow that adorned his enchanting grin, his smooth henna skin, and his twinkling truffle-colored eyes.

"Brittany, did you hear what I said?" Dimi asked while rubbing my arm.

"Hm? Wait, were you talking?"

"Good gravy woman," he sighed. "I said you can fuss me out as much as you'd like once we leave here."

Wow. That was a full and complete sentence and I didn't hear not one damn word of it. I thought Rosetta was doing a good job keeping me satisfied, but boy was I wrong. Dimi was so good that he knocked my sense of hearing out of my ass.

"Where are we going?" I asked, sliding my palm underneath the collar of his shirt.

"Wherever you wanna go," he hissed while holding my waist.

His warm hands gently kneaded the slope of my ass which would've been comforting if not for the very stiff appendage pressing against my thighs. I looked down and Dimi made it jump for me. I wanted to go to DrillVille, and I couldn't care less whether that was here or on the moon at that point.

"My place is only ten minutes away," he suggested in between sloppy kisses. "But we can go to yours if you prefer."

Why wait ten minutes when I had a perfectly good private office? I didn't climb that corporate ladder for nothing. So I reached for Dimi's buckle but he held my hand in place, stopping me from accessing the goods.

"I would prefer to not be made to wait," I whined. "Why can't we just do it here?"

Dimi hadn't been the only one in a dry spell except mine came with an attitude. He had been teasing me for weeks and I was ready to put my assumptions about his BDE to the test. Especially after that head.

"Because I've thought about fucking you everyday for seven years straight, and I have a very specific vision for our first time that doesn't include paperclips, financial reports, or silence," Dimitrius confessed with a tight jaw.

"Oh," I whispered. "In that case, your place works great."

6
WHAT'S A WHITE CHRISTMAS?

Dimitrius

When I planned all this out six months ago, I thought I would be nervous as hell for this part. Hell, any nigga would be anxious in Brittany's presence. She put the B in bad. Don't get me wrong, I was still sort of nervous to bring Brittany back to my place because the Home and Gardenesque style of her office was immaculate compared to my preferred lived-in look. But outside of that I was ready.

Truthfully I'd been ready since she dipped her finger in my drink a week ago. Most of my free time was spent thinking about what I'd do to her and how we'd celebrate after. Everything worked out the way I hoped.
Except for the office head.
I didn't plan that. I didn't plan on touching her at all in that building and for good reason. It had been years since I felt the touch of a woman and my brain had been going haywire since that sweet taste of human intimacy.
"Dimi, do not run that light. There are cameras," Brittany admonished.
"But the street is empty," I pouted.
"It's a moving violation."
"Is it?"
It was, but I didn't care. I did care about Brittany's comfort, however, so I waited the excruciating 90 seconds for the light to change. The gas pedal hit the floor as soon as I saw green. It's funny because I never considered myself impatient. I once waited in line for a pair of kicks for four hours. I regularly volunteered to catch later flights when asked. Plus I even grew rosemary from a seed once, but smelling Brittany on my skin was driving me batshit crazy, and I think it was because I wanted her for so long before I finally got her that each additional moment spent waiting felt like pins and needles agony.

If not for risk of a sex offender charge, I might have pulled over and fucked her on the street. But luckily I didn't have to because she chose my place, and we were only four minutes away.
Her fingers trailed my upper thigh and it suddenly hit me.

She liked me. She wanted me. She chose me.

Even if this all went terribly wrong and we didn't make it any further, I knew I was incredibly lucky to have Brittany's consideration let alone her enthusiastic consent. Regardless of anything that happened next I was grateful for just that.

"Hey," I said, putting the car in park. "Thanks for giving me your time and vulnerability tonight."

I gently swept a curl to the side so I could peck her forehead only to hear Brittany groan afterwards.

"Are you thanking me for giving me fire head? Ugh, could you get any more perfect?" she faux whined.

"I'm far from perfect," I chuckled while rubbing her cheek with my thumb. "But I'd like to be the perfect person for you."

The air around us fell strangely quiet and I became hyper aware of my own breathing and heart rate. I hoped I didn't scare her off by doing too much. I just wanted her to know how I-

"Damnit Dimitrius," she hissed before locking me into a bruising kiss.

Well that settled it. We clearly liked each other.

I'd like to think I'm one of the better ones, but unfortunately I'm still a man. A very horny man who had warm titties pressed against him while he was getting his tongue sucked. It didn't take long for my common sense to rush down to my dick with the rest of my blood and before I knew it, I was on Brittany's side of the car, wrapping her legs around my waist.

"Dimi," she moaned softly as I trailed her neck with kisses. "Inside."

Shit, she didn't have to tell me twice. My dick was throbbing so bad that I thought I might bust in my pants. I immediately reached for my belt buckle but Brittany stopped me with a gentle smile before I could free myself.

"I meant inside the house, baby," she clarified.

"Oh," I said, resting my forehead against hers with a chuckle. "My bad. I'm sorry."

Once some of my blood flow returned to my thinking facilities, I got Brittany's door and helped her out of the car. As soon as I led her up the steps, her eyes grew wide. Probably because she was seeing the physical proof of our similarities. I lived in a townhouse, so I didn't have much of a front yard, but that didn't stop me from stringing lights on every window, shrub, and ledge. I also had Candy Cane pathway stakes and a nutcracker at the front door. I had made my own wreath four years ago and that hung over the entryway with a big crimson bow similar to the ones Brittany had everywhere back at the office, while Christmas themed window clings greeted us with iridescent snowflakes and Happy Holiday wishes.

"Did you decorate all this yourself?" she asked, running her fingers over the ribbon-wrapped handrail.

"Yes."

"Really? You sure you didn't have help from your sister or something?"

"I'm actually an only child," I said, answering her real question. "But I loved Christmas since I was a kid, but we didn't celebrate it because my parents are Muslim. So as a grownup, I tend to go overboard."

"I get that," Brittany smiled. "My parents ran a no sugar household and now I have the world's biggest sweet tooth."

"So I've noticed," I said, pushing open the door.

That was the first thing I noticed about Brittany. Which is why I had bought a pan of cinnamon rolls from her favorite bakery for later tonight. I'm pretty sure I had indebted my left kidney to Sam, but damn, was it worth it.

"It's beautiful in here," Brittany cooed softly while discarding her coat.

Her eyes traveled between the family photos on the wall, the nine foot tree, and my reading nook which I had also decked out for Christmas. I saw a small nod of approval when she spotted my elf on the shelf, but when she focused on the star atop the tree her eyes sparkled, and my heart skipped around in my chest like a pair of kids playing hopscotch.

"Yeah it is," I agreed with my eyes trained on her.

I couldn't look away and she caught me gawking. A month ago that might've spelled the end for me, but tonight it granted me the pleasure of seeing a mischievous smile and those hooded puma eyes I've always dreamed about.

"Unzip me?" she asked.

"Absolutely," I nodded.

Brittany turned and faced the mirror near the couch so I could access her zipper. I appreciated that it was low on her back because it gave me an excuse to squeeze her hip under the guise of support, especially since I took my time. The small piece of metal hardware whined under the force of my downward pull, slowly revealing creamy brown skin that was sparsely dotted with beauty marks. With Brittany's back completely exposed to me, I flattened my palm against her spine to explore the planes of her soft shoulders and sonsy love handles. Once I had my fill, I moved on to let my fingertips trace the lines of the monarch butterfly tattoo etched against the skin of her lower back.

"You're really pretty," I grumbled lowly while placing a kiss against the curve of her neck.
"You're not even looking at my face," she chuckled.
I kissed the space between her shoulder blades where she had the most marks and she inhaled sharply, the sound almost a hiss. That was also pretty.
"Prettiness isn't limited to your face," I replied with a smile.

With most of her dress pooling around her hips, I gave it a quick downward tug to completely free her before helping her step out of it.
"Thank you," she groaned in relief while turning to face me.
My eyebrows shot up to my forehead when I looked at the mounds on her chest.
"Are your titties taped up?" I asked, seeing gauzy brown bandages in place of where I expected areola to be.
"Yes, Dimi," she said, while loosening the tape. "It works better than a strapless bra for certain dresses."
"Good to know," I replied, cataloging that knowledge for later.

Brittany freed her boobs with minimal fuss and then I discarded her titty prison in the kitchen trash. I wanted to give her time to snoop and make herself comfortable so

I put together a refreshment tray. Not even five minutes later I heard her sit on the couch. I was excited to hear what questions she had about her brief observations, but my brain still hadn't reconciled with the casual fact that there was a naked woman in my living room. All she was doing was rubbing the heel of her left foot and I got one of the most aggressive erections of my life. So much for conversation.

Luckily I wasn't far gone enough not to notice her foot was tender after dealing with heels for five hours.

"Here, let me rub them for you," I offered while placing the tray on the table. "I got some mint and jasmine massage oil a few weeks ago I've been wanting to try."

"On the couch?" she gasped. "It's high-pile chenille. Oil will definitely stain it."

"It's concerning that your fabric knowledge is so accurate," I laughed before kissing her forehead.

She snorted in response and that little sound made my heart thump. But then she tried to hide her mouth and I wasn't a fan. So I swatted away her insecurity, cupped her face in both my hands, and took the time to stroke her soft cheeks with the pads of my thumbs. Her eyes watched mine the entire time, her pupils growing wider with every lingering touch. Eventually they grew so wide that I could see my own desire shimmering in the center of her eyes, and that prompted me to be direct.

"How about the bed then?" I offered.

"I'd like that," she purred in response.

I'm 37 years old, but when I led Brit up the steps, I felt like a teenager sneaking a girl into his room for the first time. I couldn't explain it but the anticipation brewing in my belly was nostalgic. It reminded me that this was new despite the fact that I'd been daydreaming about it for years.

"Welcome to my room," I said awkwardly, displaying the space with a wave.

To be fair, my room looked better than most single men's did. I had a standing lamp in the furthest corner with my bird of paradise right next to it, there was a good amount of art on the walls, my tv was mounted against the wall, freeing up the top of my dresser for cologne and other toiletries, and my bed was made up with linens that actually matched. I thanked my Mama everyday for teaching me how to make functional space look good, because after seeing Devin's room I had nightmares.

"Don't tell me you're nervous, Dimi," Brittany giggled as I played with my thumbs.

"Have you looked in the mirror lately? Of course I'm nervous."

"Don't be. I like your room," she affirmed while kissing my forehead.

I also thanked my Mama everyday for passing me her stature, because without it I'm sure these forehead kisses wouldn't hit the same.

"Ok. My feet really do hurt. Where do you want me?" Brittany asked.

"Wherever you're comfortable."

"What about here?" she said, settling into the center of my mattress.

The comforter molded around her curves like liquid, effortlessly clinging to the shape of her. I didn't have many expectations for the night, but I knew for sure I'd never be able to look at my bed the same way after her. Brittany Barnes was going to rearrange my entire life.

"That's perfect," I whispered.

Brittany stretched her endless legs across the bed so she could rub her feet together and then all the apprehension evaporated from my body. The nerves could wait until our wedding day, we needed to unwind right now. I grabbed the oil out of the nightstand and broke the seal. The scent of sweet peppermint mixed with jojoba oil flooded my nose and I was ready to find out how it mixed with Brittany's pheromones, but she had spotted something in my drawer that made her shriek.

"What's this?" she asked while pulling out the red and white fur-trimmed cap.

"Would you believe me if I told you it was a bonnet?"

"Wait, seriously?"

"Mhm, it's satin lined. Check the inside."

"Oh, you're in deep," she said, running her fingers over the interior.

"Yeah, I know," I sighed.

I expected Brittany to recoil slightly after finding out that the man she was interested in had a Santa hat bonnet but instead she gave me a curious smirk.

"You should put it on," she purred.

"Oh, you're into that?" I chuckled while doing exactly what she asked.

"Yeah, you're not the only one who's in too deep. I've always wanted to personally hand out cookies to Santa."

My dick did a jig in my pants while I processed Brittany's admission. That meant she was also a Christmas freak and I was about to get my Ho, Ho, Hoe on big time.

"I just want you to know that I've never been more turned on in my entire life," I whispered.

"Same, although it would be better if you rubbed my feet," she giggled.

I chuckled in response to her demand, but I made no mistake about it, I knew it was a demand.

"I like that you're bossy," I confessed, kneeling before her.

She gave me a soft, lip-biting smile before I brought her feet into my lap and made small, tight circles on her heels, encouraging her worn muscles to loosen and relax. It didn't take long for the pressure of my thumb to make them do just that, and when I felt the tension bleed from her heels, my strokes spread from her heel to the soles of her pretty feet. Which to my surprise made her moan.

I loved hearing her moan.

It sent sparks racing down the length of my spine every time, and I became hyper-focused on making her do it again.

Because I was definitely going to make her do it again.

With my interests secured, I begin rolling my fingertips over the bottom of Brittany's toes. Her head lolled back softly and her eyelids fluttered from enjoyment, but she kept her lips pursed tight. I let my fingers trail up the back of her calf, still keeping my circles broad and rhythmic, and that earned me a pleased sigh.

But not a moan.

That was fine though because her body betrayed her.

Every time I inched forward, Brittany melted further into

the bed. So I moved in pursuit of perfection, gliding upward every few seconds until I reached the one spot that was guaranteed to make her moan with abandon. I played with her cat with that same soft rhythm while taking her freshly oiled toes into my mouth, then finally I got what I wanted. The sweetest sound known to man:

Brittany Barnes completely uninhibited.

Brittany

Finding out you were right about something is a high like no other. It's reassuring, it fills you with confidence, and you get bragging rights if asked about it. However fucking around and finding out was a different story, and I feared I may have done the latter while watching Dimi suck my toes like they were slathered in hot honey.

He was nasty all right.

White people taco night nasty.

"I'm glad that oil is edible," Dimi said with a smile. "It worked out."

"Take your clothes off now," I grunted.

My head was spinning like I was underwater because I was still recovering from my third orgasm, but I knew enough to know I wanted another, and I wanted it soon.

"Say please," Dimi barked back.

"Take. It. Off," I growled.

He said he liked that I was bossy and I was about to make him eat his words. He locked gazes with me and I stared back. We stayed that way for at least half a minute before Dimi's lips curled into a sly smile. I smirked in return because I expected him to yield, but instead of moving to strip he placed both his arms on the side of me to cage me in while his very stiff length pressed into my center. I instinctively curled my hips forward to feel more of him but he pinned me in place with the strength of his legs. "Santa said say please," he gritted.

I don't know how it was possible but his voice rewired my brain. I wanted to be irritated that someone was making demands of me, but instead I found myself wanting to comply.

"Please, Dimitrius," I whimpered.

Dimi's lips eased back into a playful smirk that sent my heart thumping.

"That's all you had to say, pretty girl," he said, kissing the corner of my lips.

He peeled off his layers with efficiency, keeping his eyes on mine the entire time. This was the second time I'd ever seen Dimi in something other than his signature dress shirt/tie combo and I was thoroughly enjoying the show. Especially when just his pants remained.

"You have tattoos," I gasped when I saw the ink on his right shoulder.

A set of delicate watercolor stars glistened against his defined delt. With the rich Violet highlighting the natural red undertones present in his skin.

"Just one," he said, tugging at his belt. "It's a constellation representing Cassiopeia, the queen of fate. I got really into mythology and astrology in undergrad."

His pants and briefs fell to the ground unceremoniously and I hissed in a ragged breath at the full sight of him. Dimi being short never bothered me, but now I knew where the extra height had gone.

"What's wrong, Brit?" Dimi cooed.

He must have noticed I was avoiding his gaze, but I was told to never look a horse directly in the eyes. It could spook them.

"Um, nothing," I lied.

"Brittany," he sighed.

"It looks like a prayer candle," I confessed. "Where is that supposed to go?"

"Well if I remember correctly from the car, you wanted it inside."

"I may have been overly ambitious due to an incomplete asset report."

"No, I don't think so. I think you can handle anything thrown your way with proper preparation and a little support," Dimi whispered while hovering over me.

His middle finger toyed with my sensitive clit before his lips sought mine in a succession of soft, intimate kisses. Preparation, meet support.

But I was greedy so it wasn't enough.

I pulled his body into mine, hoping to rub his hard length against my slit. However, I forgot about our slight height difference and the uncoordinated movement pressed his tip to my entrance. Precum beaded on Dimi's head, ready to be of assistance and that probably should've been the point that I stopped and regained some self control. Unprotected sex was worse than crack according to the abstinence based sex-ed I had to suffer through in high school.

For some reason though I still listened to my impulses

and widened my legs to let him slip inside.
Sorry Mrs. Shepley.

I was right to be initially concerned because, God, that
was a tight fit. So tight that I almost came immediately,
and he was only a third of the way in. Dimi's eyes flooded
with the most intense look of pleasure before they fluttered shut. He gathered the sheets in between clenched
fists while his breath deepened with a measure of control
I'd only seen and utilized during guided meditation or
yoga. I tried to grind against him but he pinned my hips
in place with one hand, silently shaking his head no.

"Brittany, are you sure you're ok with this?" he asked. "I
have condoms."
Condoms were normally a smart choice, but Dimi didn't
seem eager to grab one and I wasn't loving the idea of him
exiting me to do so either.
"I'm on birth control, I get tested every three months, and
I trust you. Are you ok with this?" I replied.
Dimi's eyes finally reopened with his hazy dilated pupils
locking into mine. He freed my left hip from the weight
of his hand then gently stroked my cheek for a few seconds before his sightline traveled down to our point of
connection.
"Yes," he gruffed. "But this is not what people mean when
they say they're dreaming of a white Christmas."
"Semantics," I moaned, as we began to move.

Dimi filled me with long languid strokes while he stole
my breath with passionate kisses. His free hand laced
through the curls on my nape, with his scalp scratches
syncing to the countence of our thrusts. I was finally able

to sink my nails into the skin of his shoulders and the satisfaction from that achievement doubled when our movement encouraged me to rake the planes of his back. Which in turn encouraged him to pick up my hips and fuck me deeper.

"Dimitrius," I moaned. "Just like that, baby."

"I got you, sweetheart," he chuckled. "I got you, Brittany baby."

Dimi then dipped his head to pepper the curve of my neck with kisses, soft and teasing. His warm breath carried the scent of mint as it tickled my collar bones.

"I'm gonna marry you," he declared against my skin.

"Is that a threat?" I teased.

Dimi's mouth slowly trailed down to my budded nipples and he took one into his mouth while teasing the other.

"It's a promise," he grunted before switching sides.

I believed him because we were making love in the Californian moonlight. Passionate kisses turned our steady rhythm into something frantic and desperate, with both of us chasing our release together. All that friction and pressure finally overwhelmed us, and while I came with a scream, Dimi came with a whimper. His entire body twitched for a few seconds immediately after before his muscles sagged in defeat. But when I noticed he was still hard, I rolled my hips forward a few more times for good measure.

"Brittany, wait," Dimi pleaded breathlessly. "Wait, wait, wait."

Spoiler alert: I did not wait.

Which is how my knees ended up being eye level with my chest.

Everything moved tortuously slow the first time versus now, when I was getting fucked into the mattress at a 55 degree angle. I realized I bit off more than I could chew when I couldn't keep Dimitrius still enough to ease into my next orgasm. He snatched it from me violently, making me cum so hard my back arched off the bed.

"That's right, baby girl. Give me that," Dimitrius groaned while I cried for mercy.

One clearly wasn't enough, but three were plenty, and my following release came out hot and fast, which pushed Dimi over the edge for the second and hopefully final time. My coochie was spent but it was amazing to see him come undone after nearly a decade of social conservation.

"You'll pay for that," he huffed while pulling out.

Dimi rolled over next to me with a content sigh before pulling me onto his chest. The room was quiet, and the air between us carried the unmistakable aura of shared bliss.

And I had to ruin it with a joke.

"That's not very jolly of you," I said, flicking the end of his hat/bonnet.

"Hush before you get coal in your stocking," Dimi chuckled while patting my booty.

His big hand stroked the expanse of my back with such tenderness that I practically heard Maxwell crooning in the background, and I knew that was a lie.

"I doubt I'll be getting coal. My cookie so nice, it made Santa come twice."

"If you wanna count we can count, little Miss Water fountain. By the way, I didn't know I was getting the Grand

Geyser treatment."

"Did you see the necklace before you gave it to me? Of course you were getting the Geyser experience."

Dimi's lighthearted smile took on a more serious expression when I mentioned one of my presents. Almost like he was worried or something.

"In all seriousness, did you like everything? Do you want me to exchange anything?" he asked softly, voice full of nerves.

Dimi gave me twelve gifts all together, thirteen if we count the plant and the pot separately. All together I received my wish list plant, a blanket that I now couldn't live without, a mug that made slow-drinking my afternoon tea possible, a wallet that was a rarer find than the plant, a pair of glitter boots that could give MJB a run for her money, a golden egg used to store jewelry, an OG cover of Vivid by Beverly Jenkins, my birthstone necklace, two cashmere scarves, one annual coffee pass for Cool Beans, one pair of silver-set garnet earrings, and a snow globe that contained a piece of my heart.

"Now that you ask, the B necklace was really off mark," I teased. "What does that even stand for? Broccoli?"

"The B stands for Baddie," Dimi scoffed while tickling my sides. "I don't know, the ladies down at Samson's Fine Jewelry thought it was pretty nice."

"It was really nice," I chuckled honestly. "You know me scarily well."

"It's kind of hard not to take notice," Dimi cooed. "You're a once-in-a-lifetime woman."

If my blushing was visible, I would've been lit up like that big ass Christmas tree in the living room. How did I go so long without noticing how perfect he was? And why didn't I act sooner?

"Now I feel extra bad that I didn't get you anything," I murmured against Dimi's skin.
His chest vibrated with an amused hum. Something told me that my admission was probably one of the many reasons he chose to remain a secret santa.
"If you really wanna get me something, I have a request," he whispered.
A loving peck was placed on my temple. The careful gesture made me smile so hard that at that point he probably could've asked me for a personal island and I would've tried to find a way to make it happen.

"What is it?" I asked with stars twinkling in my eyes.
"I know how important Christmas day is to your folks, so I'm not asking for that. But I'd really like it if you'd spend Christmas Eve with me. We can watch all your favorite cheesy Hallmarks, drink peppermint hot cocoa, and have dinner. You wouldn't have to do a thing. I already got a chicken brining."
He was selling this hard. Movie marathons, sugar rushes, dinner. What more could a girl ask for?
"Can we kiss a little bit too?"
"I'll kiss you however much you want, wherever you'd like," Dimi smiled.

After years of mismatches, misunderstandings, and mistakes, Santa had finally slipped the perfect man under my tree. Someone who knew me, who respected me, and someone who could make me smile like a kid hopped up on laughing gas. I didn't have to try to make this work, it just did.

And all I had to say was,

"Yes."

Dimi gave me a big smile that showed all his teeth. You would've thought I just offered him the key to the city or pulled an Oprah and started handing out cars.

"Just wait until Human Resources catches wind of this," he laughed, while rolling me into a spoon. "They're gonna have a field day."

"Actually I got a friend in HR, so I think we'll be good," I teased.

"Yeah, I think so too," Dimitrius nodded.

He raised his hand to stroke my shoulder before planting a tender kiss there. A kiss that silently promised me the world.

"Happy 12th day of Christmas, Brit," he cooed.

"Happy 12th day of Christmas, Dimi," I whispered. "I can't wait for next year."

Fin.

THANK YOU!

To my reading homies:
Thank you for reading this book and others like it. Thank you for following my journey, thank you the support through recommendations, reviews, and kind words, and thank you for giving me the tools to fight another day in the sometimes cutthroat world of publishing. I love y'all with all my heart, and I can't wait to surprise both of us with what happens next.

To my friends:
Thank you for putting up with me during crunch week, and all the other weeks in between when I drop something random and often outrageous into our group chat and ask, "Does this work?" I love y'all from the bottom of my heart and I can't wait until we get this compound cracking.

To my husband:
Thank you for telling me the first cover was trash. You were right. Don't do too much though.

7
One For The Team Preview

A Happy Holidays Short

Chrissy

"About damn time!" Milly cheered.

It was no secret that Milly did not care for my relationship with Derek. When I first introduced them and asked her what she thought several days later she just said, *"If you like it, I love it."* Which we all know is code for, *"That man is trash."*

"Hopefully now you'll take Blessing fine-ass up on his **several** offers to be your man," Milly giggled.
I knew she'd bring this up, but who could blame her?

Blessing Harrell was the Minneapolis Hare's beloved center and the league's 2024 player of the year. He was 29, six foot one, and 215 pounds of lean muscle wrapped in skin so deep it almost sparkled under the stadium lights. He was objectively handsome in a real, "I'd ride his face until the New Year," kind of way. On top of being unfairly wealthy, extensively educated, and enviously kind. Obviously, he was Minnesota's most eligible bachelor. Which is why I felt inclined to tell Milly that he was **not** trying to be my man.

The reason she believed otherwise is simply because sometimes we ate our pregame together and he often extended me invitations to hang out with him and a couple of the other guys on the team. I think he was just being friendly since I was technically still kind of new with my year anniversary coming up just next week. So I often declined because of that. I didn't want to intrude on their dynamic just because he felt sorry for me, plus it used to make Derek uncomfortable.

He also swore up and down that Blessing was trying to get at me.
But me and Blessing were just friends.
Friends. Friends. Friends.
"That man does not want me," I laughed. "Anyway I gotta go. I just pulled up."
"Mhm, have a good game. Make sure you tell Blessing you're single now! Love you cousin."

"Goodbye with your messy ass," I scoffed before adding, "I love you too."
I loved Milly to death but she did not know what she was talking about. Minnesota's finest did not want me.

Blessing

The roads were clearer than a calm summer sky and it was freezing out, so the crowds weren't too heavy. But she still wasn't here.
She was late and Chrissy was almost never late.
I hoped everything was ok.
Mostly because I knew I couldn't step in and fix it. As much as I wanted to, as much as I wanted her.

When management told us our new mascot was a woman, I just knew they were going to bring in some bimbo who was all body and no talent to shake her ass in a tiny costume and boost viewership. Instead what we got was Chrissy Hawkins, a Juilliard graduate with an extensive resume and some serious athletic ability. Her dance moves did boost viewership, but it's because somehow she still found the energy to engage the crowd while lugging around that hot ass suit. She could hit a split on the ice and then hop up and high five kids passing by in the stands. While I was the official face of the team along with Bear, Davis, and Little Foot, she was the heart of it.

She was also fine as hell, but much to my dismay, she had a boyfriend. A boyfriend that she was loyal to unfortunately.
Chrissy would always try to talk, Desmond or whatever

his name was, up to me when we did our pregame catch up, but I was never impressed. He had a little bank account, no car, no ambition, and a whole lot of attitude. Always telling her what she could and couldn't do.
My daddy would call him a buster, but I'm not that well mannered.
He was a bitch in my eyes.

Chrissy deserved better, and I'd been trying to tell and or show her that for the last year, but I never had any luck. Hopefully that would change today however. Our bye week began tomorrow night and I hoped I could use that brief break to convince her to spend some time together.
Without the company of her so-called boyfriend.

"Bless, they're calling for us. Come on," Little Foot sighed.
"Just tell them I'm taking a shit or something. I need like three more minutes."
"Bless, she's probably running late."
"She never runs late," I argued.
"Never say never."
I knew Little Foot was probably right. Chrissy was likely running late, but something told me if I waited just a little longer I could find out why. And just before L could drag me off to the locker rooms, Chrissy came bounding in.

Her coffee hued skin shimmered under the dim fluorescent lights like the manifestation of magic. Her hips swayed with each quick stride, encouraging her freshly braided hair to swish against her back, and her nutmeg brown eyes glowed with new determination. She was so determined that she almost breezed right past me. But I stopped her with a gentle tap on the shoulder before she could get too far.

"Hey, Chrissy," I beamed warmly, interrupting her dark cloud.
"Hey, Bless. I'm sorry I didn't see you at first. I'm just kind of in my own head."
I could tell. She looked irritated. Angry even.
"Is everything ok?" I asked.
Please say no. Please say no. Please say no.
"It's nothing," she sighed.
Damn, so much for hope.
"I just broke up with my boyfriend."
How often is God good? You better answer all the time. I almost broke into a full praise dance hearing that it had finally happened. I prayed for that niggas downfall everyday. Won't he do it!

"Oh no," I said, bringing my hand to my mouth to feign distress. "What happened?"
"We just got into a disagreement about my job," she pouted.
"Why, did he think something's going on between us?"
I hope he did. While the other two were respectful, I didn't try to hide the way I felt about Chrissy. I wanted him to know this wasn't the place to get comfortable. His girl worked for the NHL and niggas were creeping.
"He always thinks that. But no, I've told him that we're just friends," she laughed, waving a pretty manicured hand in dismissal.

Friends? No.

 I didn't want to suck a fart out of my friend's asshole. I didn't hold games up for friends. I didn't get jealous and want to give my friends the whole wide world and everything in it.

"I'm not your friend, Chrissy," I said firmly, letting my eyes drag over her soft body.

Her expression told me she was distraught over my admission but her body language said something different. Her bottom lip puckered with a questioning pout, while her ample chest poked out ever so slightly, inviting me to step closer. I wasn't one to turn down an invitation so I moved close enough to smell the sweet cocoa butter lingering on her skin. She smelled better than I imagined she would which is crazy considering her scent reminded me of the bougie ass bakery in Downtown East. But that was just the magic of Chrissy Hawkins.

"Wait, what?" she squeaked, finally realizing what I said.

"I'm. Not. Your. Friend," I repeated, tipping her chin upward so I could stare into her eyes.

Chrissy leaned forward slightly as if she wanted to press her lips against mine, but she hesitated for just a millisecond too long.

"HARRELL! Get your ass to the locker rooms now!" Coach hollered, interrupting the moment.

Talk about a cockblocker. His wife wasn't giving him any so now he wanted the rest of us to be miserable.

I was already on thin ice for ditching our last presser though, so I knew I couldn't push it any more than I had. But rest assured this wasn't the end of our conversation.

Chrissy was single and I was fresh off of Christmas break and about to go into another one. I had all the time in the world, and I was about to use every second of it pursuing her.

About the Author

Aria is a die-hard romantic and her main goal is to always be drying her eyes from something sickly sweet. She has been dreaming up romance stories since she was seven years old, with the first one being a Toy Story fanfic. She's also a Neo-soul and R&B enthusiast who's forever got a song stuck in her head. You can find her looking for good food, (especially ramen), reading, writing, or enjoying time with her family in her free time.

She lives happily in Saint Louis, Missouri with her middle-school-sweetheart-turned-husband and their adorably chaotic son. Her dream is to one day write inclusive stories that center BIPOC full-time, but for now, she labors in fraud as a working stay-at-home mom and a part-time social media comedian.

Also By Aria

Glory
https://www.amazon.com/dp/B0D1YH9BNH

Burry The Hatchette
https://www.amazon.com/dp/B0CT34SSS4

Candy Corn Curses
https://www.amazon.com/dp/B0DJLQ3W14

Rudy Jones's New Year's Resolution
https://www.amazon.com/dp/B0CLMWNPQJ

From Kingston, With Love
https://www.amazon.com/dp/B0CPDFXY9P

Bloom
https://www.amazon.com/dp/B0C82QWN2F

Candid
https://www.amazon.com/dp/B0BZMZVZ47

One For The Team
(Coming soon.)

8
LET'S CONNECT!

If you read and enjoyed this book, there's a chance we have other authors in common. I'd love to connect on social media!